"ARE YOU ONE OF THOSE MEN WHO LET A WOMAN DO IT ALL?"

"I've seen women who come on strong when their husbands are near and then turn cold when it's safe."

"Oh?" Idly, her fingers stirred the hair at the back of his head, tingled along his jaw, up behind his ears. She blew softly on his neck. "You think I'm one of those?"

"I think you'd enjoy the game, yes. I could die of old age waiting for the pay-off."

"You know the island. You name it. Time, place, everything. I'll meet you."

"That's enough. I'm leaving." He started to get up, but she was leaning on him, her breath warm in his ear.

"What are you afraid of, Sergeant March? I thought cops weren't afraid of anything," she said, as she slid her arms around his neck and pulled him slowly down. . . .

Other SIGNET Ellery Queen Titles

THE KILLER TOUCH

by

ELLERY QUEEN

Ⓓ

A SIGNET BOOK

NEW AMERICAN LIBRARY

TIMES MIRROR

SIGNET, SIGNET CLASSICS, MENTOR, PLUME AND MERIDIAN BOOKS
are published by The New American Library, Inc.,
1301 Avenue of the Americas, New York, New York 10019

FIRST PRINTING, JUNE, 1975

1 2 3 4 5 6 7 8 9

PRINTED IN THE UNITED STATES OF AMERICA

Cast of Characters

TRACY DUNN—A frail ethereal beauty who was needled by her husband to an addict's fate; she had been on *H* so long she didn't know there was any other letter in the alphabet................ 7

ROLF DUNN—A swaggering soldier of fortune—usually someone else's. This international mastermind couldn't kick the habit of killing after the war 13

BURTON MARCH—His idyllic vacation on a lonely island was thronged with daydreams and nightmares 15

CAPTAIN O'RYAN—An island-hopping mariner who is always on deck for a sexboat. His prepossessing build was a caution to men and a challenge to women 16

COCO—This islander's disposition was indicated by the color of his hats: white—glad; red—angry. He was wearing a blue—sad: no-guest, no-fish, no-tip chapeau 20

JOSS LEEDS—The tippling landlady of an island purgatory who disappears into her bottle as magically as a genie............................... 21

GODFREY—Dishwasher, beachboy and bellhop, he is
so rickety that his legs look like parenthesis..   25

JATA—The tall thin blue-black woman from Petit
Martinique who exists in a world of death,
blood, and black magic......................27

MAUDIE—She stuck as close and as tenaciously to
Burt as a plastic adhesive...................   27

BUNNY DEVORE—The only thing soft about this sa-
distic stripper was her brain; her specialty
dance demonstrated the symbolism of the gun   66

ACE SMITH—A hardened gunman whose modern
weapons were ineffectual against primitive rage
and vengeance   75

HOKE FARNUM—His emotionless face had the color
and texture of pie dough with the features
pressed in—but he was half-baked...........   75

PROLOGUE

She sat alone on the bed, and the kerosene lamp played its flickering shadow-light on her drawn face. Outside, the surf pounded the minutes to shreds, reducing time to a soft pulp without substance or division. She raised her hands from the writing pad on her lap and ran her fingers through her black hair. Her hands moved jerkily as though in answer to someone else's command. She felt her hair lying warm and heavy on the backs of her hands; the hair too seemed not to be a part of her. She sniffed and felt the swollen congestion inside the bridge of her nose. Moisture filmed her eyes as she looked back down at the paper, giving the dark blue lines an outline of light.

> *. . . so there seems no point in going on, dreading every tomorrow and regretting each yesterday . . .*

It sounded melodramatic, the kind of farewell a B actress would write in the hope that it would appear in the newspapers. She tore out the sheet and started another:

> *Dear Rolf,*
> *Three nights on this island and a week away from you have given me a chance to think about all that has happened and I have decided*

She drew a line through the last phrase, and added: *since I married you*. Still the letter seemed a sticky, sentimental coating on the purity of the act she was about to commit. The act wouldn't hurt Rolf. Inconvenience him, yes. Anger him even. But she could never

7

hurt him, any more than she had ever been able to please him.

Tracy gasped as pain gouged her stomach. She pressed her palms flat against it and felt the pain-taut muscle trembling beneath the skin. She touched a finger between her breasts and felt the perspiration, slick, greasy cold. *I'm getting sick, and it's too soon. I wanted to get everything done before. . . .*

She rose abruptly from the coconut-fiber mattress, belting her white terrycloth robe around her waist. She felt nervous, edgy. There were flashes at the edge of her vision. The stone wall of the room had an unpleasant glow; the furniture was haloed. Overhead, the thatched roof crawled with shadow-life. She heard rasping noises, creaks, murmuring voices in a distant room.

But there is only one room and the other cabins are empty . . .

She carried the lamp onto the lean-to veranda, her rubber sandals grating on the sand-strewn concrete floor. A breeze struck the lamp, causing it to dip low and send up a gray spiral of smoke. She adjusted the wick and set the lamp on a hand-hewn table beside a stack of mold-smelling magazines. *Fate, Astrology, Your Future. . . .* The nearsighted woman who owned the island supplied her guests with the kind of reading she herself liked. Joss at least believed in something.

A soldier crab tried to scuttle beneath her feet, clattered against the table, then folded its claws and lay still. Tracy toed the unresisting object across the floor, opened the screen door, and kicked it out onto the sand. She watched the crab stick out an exploratory claw, turn itself upright, then scuttle away into the night. She stepped out onto the sand and glanced right, then left. The adjacent cabins were dark and silent. Palms rustled overhead, and a tinny cha-cha beat came from the direction of the beach club. The boys had turned in Radio Trinidad on their battery set. No doubt the cleaning women had already locked themselves in their shack, and Joss would be drunk. Nobody would know, nobody would care . . .

Salt-crusted grass crunched beneath her feet as she walked toward the sea. She thought of frost on the churchyard on Sunday morning, walking in patent-leather shoes with her mother and father on either side, smelling respectively of perfume and shaving lotion. Then the odor of ancient varnish biting her nostrils, and the woody-musty smell of the song book in her hands. She had loved to sing hymns, sending her voice out among the others and having it return . . . a hundredfold. She'd liked that, and the part about casting your bread upon the waters. . . .

Her mind returned to the aching stiffness in her joints. Railroad vines snatched at her bare ankles as she walked toward the phosphorescent surf. When she reached the sand she kicked off her sandals and walked barefoot. Once she'd loved to feel warm sand against her feet; now it was only an irritation, and even the air felt unpleasant on her face, like spiders crawling. Her nose ran and her eyes watered. She had a terrible awareness of the flesh clinging to her bones, of each joining of cartilage, muscle, and tissue; of her brain lying overhead, each movement causing pain to flare up behind her eyes.

Hate my body, hate it hate it hate it.

The sea lay like a pall of smoke, inviting.

The prickly weight of the bathrobe was gone. She left the clothing lying on the sand like dead skin, diseased and discarded. The water was exactly the temperature of the air; it was a pressure on her legs and no more. She stumbled over a rock and barnacles gouged her knees like cinders. She climbed over the reef, felt the coral cut into her feet, and told herself it didn't matter.

The sea was high. A wave swelled up, towered overhead, then collapsed and buried her in greenness. It wasn't water, it was raw force tearing her apart, lifting her body high and slamming it down, dragging her across an object which raked her body with long sharp claws, then leaving her to gasp on the reef. It lifted her again, higher and higher, swinging her in a silken ham-

mock. She relaxed, feeling relief from the pull of muscle in her shoulders, stomach and chest; she drew in a
deep breath and waited for her lungs to fill with
water—

Air came in.

She opened her eyes and found herself on the sand.
A bubbling carpet of surf came forward, buried her,
and left her again. Oh, I didn't know it was so hard to
drown. If only I could swim, I could go far out . . .

She was tired. She lay there and let the air dry her
body. After a time she rose and dressed. The surf
teased, bubbling forward, hissing back.

Back at the cabin, she carried the lamp into the
bathroom. She smelled the salty-musty odor of old
swim suits, and heard the drip-drip-drip of the
shower-head which hung like a drooping rusty blossom.
She set the lamp on the low stand beside the washbasin
and peered at the warped and mottled image in the
mirror. She felt a curious, cold detachment toward herself. The upward glow of the lamp shadowed her forehead with the arch of her brows, unplucked and heavy
in the center. Her nose seemed long and thin, and the
white crescent scar on its tip looked more prominent
than ever. Her wet hair lay flat on her skull and framed
her narrow face like a cowl. High cheekbones shaded
her eyes, and the line of her jaw lent her cheeks a hollow aspect.

You're dying, Tracy.

"I've been dying ever since I married him."

She said it aloud, and felt dismay at the thin sound
of her voice. She filled her lungs to produce a deeper
resonance; her breasts rose and brushed against the
cloth, causing a shiver to spread throughout her body.
She gave a shudder which rejected all clothing; her skin
seemed raw all over; the robe was an unbearable
weight on her shoulders, and the band of her shorts
was a hand squeezing her in two.

She closed her eyes, and the lids grated like fine
sand. She pressed her fingertips against her eyes, felt

the eyeballs rolling beneath the lids like grapes. Got to
hurry, she thought, before I get too sick—

She got her safety razor from her toilet case, grasped
the rust-rimmed blade between her thumb and forefin-
ger. Her hands began to shake. The third try produced
a cut which barely broke the skin. She sat down on the
stool, breathing heavily.

If I only had a cap, just enough to get straight. . . .

Stupid. You left your purse on the boat and it's not
due back until tomorrow.

Tomorrow! What about *now?*

Maybe you can find some. You had stuff squirreled
everywhere.

Again she searched the lining of her clothes. Her lipstick tube. Compact. Fingers of her gloves. Face powder—

Her fingers touched something round, oblong. Joy
dissolved her strength, and a small sob escaped her lips.
She picked out the gelatin capsule and blew the face
powder from its surface. A full one, sure. Rolf always
got full measure. The pushers knew better than to hand
him fogged caps. Not that Rolf would mind being
cheated. He treated everybody with a studied careless-
ness, half-hoping someone would cheat and give him an
excuse.

She separated the two halves of the capsule and
dumped the contents onto a sheet of paper. Her body
shivered, and she could feel moisture from her nose
poised on her upper lip. Her fingers seemed gnarled,
blunt and clumsy, but they were steady as she used the
razor blade to scrape the powder into a tiny windrow
at the edge of the paper. She dumped the powder into
a spoon, then held the spoon above the chimney of
the lamp until there was only a clear liquid. She took
the needle from her suitcase, filled it, and watched the
liquid climb the spike. While it cooled she took off the
belt of her bathrobe and wrapped it around her leg
just above the knee. It was easier in the arm but there
was already a string of purple dots like a fading
tattoo. . . .

Now the vein throbbed, swollen purple. With flawless rhythm the glass bird swooped down and thrust its glittering steel beak into the knotted worm of the vein. Its glass intestine filled with thick red blood, blended with the fluid inside and became pink. Her thumb pressed down and the fluid disappeared. . . .

Ah . . .

Warmth in her chest, like an explosion of pleasure. It rippled along her skin; her lips spread in a loose smile and a faint breathy giggle escaped them. Finally she withdrew the needle and laid it on the stand. A fly came to drink of the glistening red droplet which hung from its tip. She regarded it with a benevolent smile. Get high, little fly. After a long time she carried the lamp into the bedroom and sat down on the bed. The room seemed to flatten out and relax like a cat stretching itself before a fire. Before it had been a jangling, jarring chaos of corners and angles; now it was exactly right, and there was beauty in each joining of stone. The air was filled with streamers of light, rose, purple, green and blue; they wove themselves into a net and enveloped her, swinging her gently. Smoke curled from the lamp like a satin ribbon edged with purple and orange. She felt a gratitude for the lamp and then no gratitude; she was the lamp, the house, the sea and the universe, all joined in one.

But . . .

Someone was standing in the door behind her. She fought to ignore it, knowing that if she came down she could never go as high again.

"Tracy."

Rolf's voice. How had he got here? What does he want? I'll push him out of my mind, not even think about him . . .

But the effort of holding herself high caused her to lose it. She felt herself coming down, down.

"Please, Rolf," she spoke without turning. "Later we can talk."

"Just struck yourself, did you, baby? All squared now, eh?"

"Mmmm."

"What are you writing?"

A hand appeared from behind her shoulder. It seemed almost to be hers, except for the long spatulate fingers. The square-cut diamond on his little finger caught the lamplight and sent yellow shards flashing around the room. She would have enjoyed the diamond universe, but Rolf was reading her letter. Why did he read aloud?

"You've decided what, Tracy? What have you decided? Suicide? You've mentioned it enough."

Round rolling words like lumps of cold gravy dripping on her head. She knew the answers but there were more important questions, and each question had its own answer.

His hand grasped hers and held it under the lamp. She heard him laughing. "You couldn't do it, could you? Not while you had your needle. I counted on that." He released her hand. "How do you know death isn't the same thing, Tracy, only better? How do you know death isn't the biggest fix of all?"

He turned her to face him; he must have done it roughly because she felt pain somewhere behind the soft pillowing pleasure. She lowered her head, but he lifted her chin and met her eyes.

"Look at me, Tracy. You know something funny?"

She wondered if it was the lamplight which made his face seem molded in wax. Even the blond mustache looked like the ones they put on department store dummies. But the pale blue eyes were real; they held a look of amused pity as though he had somehow learned the hour of her death.

The eyes didn't change when he slapped her.

"Answer me, Tracy. You know what's funny about your trying to kill yourself?"

She looked out of a long dark tunnel; she was hidden up high behind her eyes, protected by the hard helmet of her skull. She would stay here quietly, warm and cozy, where he couldn't hurt her.

He slapped her again, then again. The waxy mask

seemed to crack and fall away, leaving a wizened old man's face. His hands encircled her throat, and she realized abruptly there was no use hiding inside her skull. There was no air. She clawed at his hands, and up inside her brain the cells began blinking off like lights at bedtime.

ONE

Burt March sat on a coil of rope and watched the green-yellow islands of the Grenadines sail past. The schooner wallowed through a heavy sea, but there was no wind and the sails were furled. From below came the intermittent growl of the diesel engine; an occasional vile whiff of exhaust fumes reminded Burt of the city he'd left the day before.

He gazed around the open deck, crowded with islanders returning from St. Vincent after selling their vegetables, pigs and chickens. A rum bottled passed from one black hand to another; a Negro girl flashed him an over-the-shoulder look, then reached into her basket and tossed him a ripe mango. He caught it and smiled at her; she turned quickly to whisper to a girl who sat beside her. Their burst of tinkling laughter pleased him; he was glad to leave the grit and sticky July heat of Florida, to forget the pinch of a shoulder holster, and to be among people who didn't know him as Dective Sergeant Burton March of the Crystal City Police Department. He hated the puffed, indignant faces of solid citizens, the uneasy look from those who had nothing to fear from him, and the pinched, scared faces of those who did. He hated the scared faces most, maybe because he knew others in the department who liked them scared.

A boy picked his way across the deck, collecting fares. Burt drew out his wallet and removed a British West Indian dollar. "I get off at Isle de Trois."

"I think we don't stop there, sir."

Burt looked up. The boy was shirtless and barefoot, with trousers cut off at the knees. "Why not?"

"Too much sea. The water very swift there, no good bottom to hold anchor."

"Well, can you get me in close? Joss could send out a boat to pick me up."

The boy nodded. "I ask the captain."

As the boy started away, Burt called, "How old are you?"

"Fourteen year." The boy squinted at Burt for a moment, then shrugged and started up the gangway.

Burt sighed and pulled a paperback book from the pocket of his white canvas trousers. *The same age.* Funny. And the kid that got sick on the plane looked around fourteen, too. Burt remembered the smell of fear in the darkened store, the roar of the other's gun and the ripping pain in his thigh, then his own reflexive shot at the muzzle flash. He saw again the beardless face, curiously feminine in death, and the ugly redness where Burt's slug had torn through his throat. . . .

Burt closed the book and returned it to his pocket. There would be time to read on the island, time to dive in the air-clear water, fish, and walk on the salt-white sand and put strength in his leg, or just to sit at the top of the island's lone hill and think. What about? Well, think about reaching the age of twenty-eight and deciding you've picked the wrong career. That would keep him busy for his entire month of sick leave. He wondered if he should've sent Joss a wire . . . but then she'd told him once that nobody came during the summer. He'd probably have the whole square mile of the island to himself.

The boy returned and said the captain wanted to see him. Burt planted his bamboo cane and rose. He was slightly less than six feet tall, heavy-set in a hard-muscled way which made him look average. He used the cane no more than necessary to steady himself on the rolling deck.

The wheelhouse swarmed with girls in bright-colored dresses. It was a mark of status for a girl to ride with the skipper, and Captain O'Ryan was notoriously free with his favor. He was a blue-black Negro who walked softly, talked slowly, and had a barrel-chested build.

He grinned as Burt entered. "Mister March. I din' recognize you when you board. Man, you pale, lose weight." He gripped his jaw to indicate hollow cheeks.

Burt held up his cane. "Had a little accident, so they handed me an extra vacation."

"So you rest with Miss Joss, eh? If she leave you be. Maybe I stop off one day when the sea calm down, bring some rum." O'Ryan looked at the deck, dipping and swaying below, then raised his eyes to the southeastern horizon. "I think a hurricane trying to work up." He looked sideways at Burt. "You never been in one of our hurricanes?"

"No."

"Ah, man, they come rare and small, but hard, hard." He grinned as though looking forward to it. "Well, we get you close and see if Miss Joss will pick you up. You give her something for me?"

"Sure," said Burt, then frowned as O'Ryan drew a smart, olive-green leather purse from beneath the binnacle. "That doesn't belong to Joss."

"No, a lady left it on my ship three days ago. She staying now with Joss."

A twinkle in O'Ryan's eye gave new significance to the expensive look of the purse and the seductive scent which rose from it. Burt suspected that if O'Ryan fulfilled his promise to stop on the island, it wouldn't be to visit Burt.

"Pretty lady, huh?"

"Pretty, yes, but—" O'Ryan frowned. "Her eyes move about like butterflies, never still." He shrugged and turned back to the wheel as the schooner approached a cluster of islands. "But you all that way, man, you live too fast up there."

Back on deck, Burt sat on his coil of rope and dangled the purse thoughtfully between his knees. He felt an irritating urge to peer inside and learn something more about the girl. If he dropped it, perhaps it would spring open . . .

Put it away, March. You're off-duty. Forget it.

He set it on the deck between his feet, then braced himself as the schooner heeled over abruptly. They were negotiating the swift frothy channel between two islands. Ten yards away a black jagged rock thrust up from the sea, bird droppings melting down its side like cake frosting. The schooner dipped, then soared sickeningly. It poised for a second, tilted, slid into the trough. There was a shuddering thump against the hull. A wall of white water plumed up and arched overhead. Burt put his head between his knees and felt the water drum against his back. Another swoop, a dip, and another shower, smaller than the first, the schooner righted itself and entered smooth water. Burt settled back and looked at the people sprawled on the streaming deck. A few of the girls were rising to their knees, throwing their dripping hair off their foreheads and, with a total lack of self-consciousness, raising their dresses and wringing out the water. Burt felt his feet squishing inside his white crepe-soled sneakers and decided that getting soaked was a part of inter-island travel, not at all unpleasant.

"Oh-oh, the purse. He looked down, felt a twinge of alarm, then saw it caught in a loop of rope, half-submerged in the runoff water. He picked it up and shook off the water. Better see if any got inside . . .

He paused with his hand on the catch, then shrugged.

The smell struck him again as he opened the purse; an exciting smell of perfume. Ladies' soft leather wallet. . . . Once started, he fell into an unconscious search pattern. The wallet's plastic windows contained a social security card issued to Miss Tracy Dunn, and a Florida driver's license for Mrs. Tracy Keener. Must have quit work after she got married, otherwise she'd have had her card changed. Age, twenty-eight. Well, well, she's a Gemini too, and the same age. Address in North Miami. Evidence was stacking up. Her married status didn't seem very important, since she'd come to the island alone. Where was Mr. Keener? Dead, divorced, separated, working . . . having a ball elsewhere. Weight one-oh-five, height five-four. A good build, provided the weight was arranged properly. Hair black, eyes brown. Folder of traveler's checks, all fresh and new. Whee! Hundreds, tens of 'em. Poor little working girl struck it rich. Probably married the boss's son, or the boss ... Funny no pictures, probably meant she had no kids. Lipstick, bright red, a little garish for Burt's taste. Well, nobody's perfect, Can of talcum power, funny thing to carry in a purse. Or was it? He took it out and shook it, felt a soft rattle against his hand. Maybe the powder had gotten wet and lumpy ...

The lid came off with a hard twist of his fingers. He shook out some powder and a capsule dropped into his palm. He felt a coldness at the back of his neck. He looked up quickly. The passengers were busy drying themselves. He cleaned off the capsule and saw the white powder inside. He didn't bother taking it apart. What else comes in capsules which you have to hide inside a talcum powder can? There were fourteen in all. The girl had a heavy, heavy habit. ...

He put everything back in the can, replaced the lid, returned the can to the purse and closed it. She'd been nervous as a cat, and why not? Carrying a couple hundred bucks worth of heroin. But then, to walk off the boat and leave it ...

Isle de Trois jutted abruptly from the sea to the south, humped up to a five-hundred foot prominence, then sloped gently to the north. As the schooner neared, Burt could make out the three black crags which gave the island its name. The upper slope was clothed in cedar, frangipani and shoulder-high citronella grass. At the water's edge a line of palm trees overhung the thatched roof of the beach club. In front of the club curved a silver-white beach strewn with conch shells and bleached coral. A gentle swell disturbed the lagoon and caressed the beach.

Burt had first seen the island from the deck of a cruise ship five years ago. He had recognized a scene he'd dreamed of years before, while his breath froze on the fringe of a parka, his finger stuck to an icy trigger and his eyes squinted across a frozen Korean landscape. He'd spent his last five vacations on the island, and while Caribbean prices had ballooned, Burt still paid the same as he had on his first visit: thirty dollars a week.

The schooner stopped fifty yards outside the semicircle of black rocks which enclosed the lagoon like the jaws of a giant beartrap. Burt stood at the rail listening to the grinding complaint of the engines as they fought the current which hissed and gurgled around the ship. A black figure clad in shorts moved languidly across the beach, dragged a tiny blue rowboat into the water, and started rowing across the lagoon. Burt recognized Joss's boatman, Coco. He was a skilled fisherman who knew every submerged rock within five miles of the island. Muscles corded in his powerful arms as he left the lagoon and entered the current. Five minutes later the boat thumped against the hull.

"Mist' March," he said, holding the boat steady as Burt clambered down. "I din' expect you this time."

There was no time for conversation; Burt took his bulky canvas suitcase from the cabin boy, settled into the forward thwart, and helped push off. When they reached the peace of the lagoon, Burt saw that Coco wore a blue straw hat. The boatman had two other hats, one painted red, the other white. He changed them according to his mood: white when he felt good, blue when he was sad, and red when he was angry.

"Why the blue hat?" asked Burt.

The boy spoke abruptly between strokes. "No guest. No fish. No tip."

"The woman who's staying here doesn't fish?"

"Woman?" Coco's expression of disgust encompassed the entire sex. "I never take woman to fish. Too much play, too much talk."

"She talks a lot, eh?"

"She? Man, I never see her. She remain in her cabin all day, walk the beach at night."

Frowning, Burt opened the side pocket of his bag

and took out two rolls of film. "Here's some new high-speed film. I guess you've still got that Brownie I gave you."

"Yes." Coco grinned. "Now I maybe change my hat, take you to catch big fish."

Coco tied up at a rickety jetty of poles and wood planks. It was attached to an unfinished concrete jetty begun by Joss's fourth or fifth husband—who had also inaugurated a yacht basin, a hotel, and a new clubhouse, only to abandon the island and depart with a female guest from Barbados. He'd never come back, and Joss had never continued any of his projects.

Burt stepped off the jetty and looked around. Nothing ever changed here; it could have been five years ago. He saw a figure floating at the south end of the lagoon, where the palms arched down and dipped their fronds in the surf. It could have been a corpse, it floated so still, so bonelessly complaisant to each ripple of water. But Burt recognized the mistress of the island, Jocelyn Leeds.

"Joss!"

No response. After fourteen years on the island, Joss was capable of falling asleep in the water. Her boys had to watch that she didn't drift out to sea.

Burt started down the beach. He saw smoke trailing up from a cigarette between her lips. A glass rested on the gentle mound of her stomach.

"Hey!" he called. "Hey, Joss!"

"I'm full up," she called without removing the cigarette. "You should've had O'Ryan wait."

"Don't hand me that. Come and see what I brought you."

"Now who in the world—!" She twisted to look, but a wave broke over her face. She spat out her soggy cigarette, rolled over, and started stroking toward shore. Burt opened his suitcase, took out the green beach coat he'd brought her, and walked down to the edge of the surf. Joss rose in thigh-deep water and waded ashore. Her homemade bathing costume (it was too individualistic to be called anything else, a loose-fitting playsuit made of a cotton print) wetly outlined a figure which had once been, obviously, arrestingly full. Now, though resigning itself here and there to the pull of gravity, her shape was still good enough to draw whistles at a distance. Once she'd shown Burt an old picture of herself in a net bra and panties, both of which concealed no more than the absolute legal minimum. She'd refused to say whether she'd been a runway queen, a nightclub stripper, or a freelance exhibitionist; she drew a curtain of phony coyness over her entire past and was even vague about the number of her husbands. Burt wasn't sure whether the Englishman from whom she'd inherited the island had been her third or fourth. Her hair was the color of bleached straw except at the back of her neck and behind her ears, where traces of gray were visible among the auburn. Burt placed her age at forty-five, but wouldn't have been surprised if she turned out to be five years on either side.

She walked out of the water, squinting in his direction. She was hopelessly nearsighted but scorned glasses, saying she'd seen too much already. Burt sidestepped and slid the beach coat around her shoulders. "Now you can greet your guests decently."

"Burt March!" She gave him an impulsive hug which dampened his clothes for the second time. Then she backed off a step. "Burt, you look like hell!"

"Thanks," said Burt dryly. "You haven't changed either."

"But really. You're thin and pale, and carrying a cane . . ." Her mouth flew open. "You stopped a bullet!"

"Shhh. I'm supposed to be an insurance salesman."

"Tell me, really. Did you shoot it out with a gang?"

"Crystal City's too small to support a gang. It was just a little jewelry store robbery—"

"And you went in after them?"

"Look—" He sighed. There'd be no business transacted until Joss had the entire story. "Joss, there was only one. A kid tried to heist a ring for his sweetheart. He stole his old man's gun and broke a window. He must've panicked when I came in, I don't know. He didn't live to talk about it. He was fourteen."

"Oh—" Her eyes clouded with sympathy. "Poor Burt. Let's go up to the club and get you a drink."

She slid her arm around his waist, half-helping him through the loose sand. Burt drew no personal conclusion from this intimacy; Joss had a way of making guests feel that she'd been wistfully scanning the sea for their arrival. He suspected it was only half a pose.

When they reached his luggage, she swooped down and held up the purse. "Burt March! You've changed sides!"

"If you weren't like a grandmother to me, I'd whop you. That belongs to your guest, Mrs. Keener. She left it on the schooner."

"Oh?" Her expression froze into neutrality. "I'll have Boris take it to her."

"I'd rather take it myself."

Joss frowned, then gave a shrug of indifference which somehow failed to come off. As they stepped beneath the thatched roof of the club, she gave him a sidelong look. "Whatever happened to Caroline, the girl you brought down here last year? She told me she was trying to get you to propose."

"I almost did." Burt sat down at a rough, hand-hewn table. He kept his eyes carefully on a grackle which was strutting along the railing. "We broke it off a couple of weeks ago. She wouldn't have wanted to marry a cop."

"Now Burt, she told me—" She stopped abruptly. "Oh, I get it now. Okay, we'll forget it. Boris! Two rum punches."

Boris, whose real name was Howard Charles William, was one of the few men Burt knew who could wear a wispy goatee, a purple beret, stride on black bare feet across the plank floor of an open, thatched clubhouse, then bow from the waist with all the massive dignity of a headwaiter at the Waldorf. Burt offered him the bright Hawaiian shirt he'd brought; Boris thanked him gravely and strode behind the bar to mix the drinks.

An Isle de Trois rum punch bore no resemblance to the effete cocktails served in Barbados and Jamaica. It was a potent jolt of black rum, nutmeg, brown sugar and lime. Water had to be requested, and ice was unknown on the island. Burt forced himself to sip the heavy mixture slowly; he was anxious to get to Mrs. Keener, but irritated at his own impatience.

"What's this about being full up, Joss?"

"Oh . . ." She waved her hand vaguely. "I just meant the cabins are all rented."

"But . . . I thought Mrs. Keener was the only guest."

"Her husband's due in a few days. He reserved cabin one, and she's in number two."

"Separate cabins? Why?"

"Maybe it's that kind of marriage, or maybe one of them snores. He didn't say in his letter, and I haven't been able to get ten words out of her."

Burt frowned to himself; he wanted more information, but was reluctant to tell Joss what he already knew. "Okay, that still leaves cabins three and four."

Joss sighed and spread her hands. "A week ago I got a letter from a man named Smith. He enclosed a money order. Wanted two cabins for himself and three associates—"

"*Associates?* A man named Smith?"

She looked at him. "I know what you're thinking and you can stop worrying. If they're gay, they don't stay. But I couldn't tell that from a letter, could I? And there *are* people named Smith." She looked down at her hands. "Hell, I know it sounds fishy. But I needed the money, Burt. It's been a long summer."

"You want me to leave?"

She looked up quickly. "No! Lord no, stay in number one until Keener gets here. After that . . . well, there's my house . . ."

"I wouldn't put you out."

"I wasn't thinking of—" She stopped suddenly and stood up. "Go on, deliver your purse and then we'll have another drink. Lobster okay for supper?"

"Great," he said. He watched her walk behind the

bar, through the door which led to the kitchen. Joss seemed unusually nervous, and uncharacteristically hostile to her female guest.

Godfrey, the mulatto youth who served as dishwasher, beachboy and bellhop, was waiting beside Burt's leg. The boy was painfully bandy-legged, and as Burt followed him along the sandy path, he could see at least a foot of clearance between the knobby knees. They passed cabins four and three, in that order, and beyond them Burt could see the rollers marching in like ranks of plumed soldiers, then crashing down on the sand. It was a good day for body surfing.

Ahead, Godfrey walked beneath tall, somber manchineel trees, setting his bare feet carefully down among the sharp-husked fruits. Both the sap and the fruit were poisonous, and Joss had been advised to cut down the trees. But she had a theory that any change in nature is bound to be bad. Having seen the manicured, geometric ugliness which man had produced in his own state, Burt was inclined to agree.

Ah, here was cabin two. Now he could dispose of this purse, which was turning into a millstone around his neck.

"Godfrey." His voice was lost in the booming surf. He called louder. The boy stopped and turned. "Take the bag on to the cabin. I'm stopping here—wait, here's something." He drew out a flat packet and tossed it through the air. "Strings for your guitar. See you later."

He waited until Godfrey had gone behind the ancient gnarled banyan which separated cabins one and two, then knocked on the door. The silence stretched into a full minute before a low husky voice came from the other side.

"Who is it?"

"Burt March. I just came in on the schooner."

There was another long pause. "Really? I hope you had a pleasant voyage."

Burt frowned. There was no interest in the voice, not even idle curiosity. "Are you Tracy Keener?"

"I—what if I am?"

Her voice had taken on a tense belligerence, almost as puzzling as her lack of interest.

"Did you leave something on the ship?"

"Oh." Was that a sigh of relief? Had she expected something worse?

The door opened slowly to a width of four inches. Burt glimpsed a huge, floppy beach hat which hung down to her eyebrows. A pair of oversized sunglasses covered her face to the cheekbones, and from there to the collar of her robe was a pale leprous expanse of skin which glistened wetly. Some kind of lotion . . .

"Oh, my purse." Her white hand snaked out, clutched the purse, and pulled it inside. As the door was closing, she spoke with the stilted formality of a child suddenly remembering its manners: "Thank you. I've been terribly worried."

And that was all. The door clicked shut, and Burt felt like kicking it in. What kind of reward was that? Hell, for all he'd seen of her she could have been a Martian. Maybe she didn't know about the heroin; maybe the stuff had been a plant.

He walked quietly around the cabin and leaned against the screen door of the veranda. If she were a hypo, she'd be fixing now.

Five minutes later he heard her sandals scrape on the concrete. "Oh! You . . . what do you want now?"

He turned and saw that she still wore her all-concealing costume. The robe ended at mid-thigh and he saw that her legs were heavier than he'd expected from her description. They were thick and muscled, like those of a dancer.

He realized he had no real plan of action, no desire to do more than have a good look at her. "If you'll come to the club, I'll buy you a drink."

"No."

"You don't drink?"

"I—" She made an impatient gesture with her hand. "Look, you brought me my purse. Okay, what do you want, a reward? I'll have to get some change—"

Her voice was rising. It could have been anger, but

Burt heard an undercurrent of alarm. "I don't want a reward," he said softly. "I just thought since we're the only guests, we should get acquainted."

"Oh, well . . . later. I've got a terrible sunburn and I don't feel like—"

"Are you sick?"

She faced him a moment, her chin thrust out in what was unmistakably anger. Then she whirled and went inside, slamming the door behind her.

Jata was scrubbing out the patio when Burt reached his cabin. She was a tall, thin, blue-black woman from Petit Martinique who lived in a world of death, blood and black magic. She wore a skin bag around her neck which might have contained obeah charms, but which really held tobacco. She took the two packs of Granger pipe mixture he gave her and said morosely she hoped he would enjoy his stay.

"Las' night, moon he come up all bloody. Trouble comin', *sieur,* truly."

Burt smiled. "Where's Maudie? I brought her something."

"Look behind you, *sieur*. She follow as always."

Burt turned as Jata's daughter came through the screen door. The girl he'd first seen as a gangly, tongue-tied eleven-year-old with round violet eyes and a braid like the tail of a rat, had now acquired a brazenly buxom brown body which rolled and bounced beneath a threadbare T-shirt. In past years she'd shadowed him around the island so closely that her mother had sometimes locked her in their shack.

"Remember what you asked me to bring you?" Burt asked. "You showed me the picture in the magazine."

Maudie nodded, her round violet eyes fixed on his.

Burt opened his bag and took out the brassiere he'd brought from the States. He frowned as Maudie held it speculatively to her bosom; he'd made the purchase from last year's measurements, forgetting that Maudie was a growing girl.

After the women left, Burt changed to swim trunks and walked onto the windward side of the island. Slimy

gray rock crabs skittered away from his feet. Wet rock
trembled beneath him as a wave crashed against the
ten-foot cliff. Geysers of spray erupted from holes in
the rock and drenched him. He heard the hissing moan
as the retreating waves sucked air into underground
caverns. At night the fumaroles sounded like approaching trains, men groaning in agony or women
shrieking; you soon lost the habit of trusting your ears.

He walked back to the beach and dove into the surf.
He swam past the breakers, rolled over and floated on
his back. Gannets dive-bombed the water around him;
pelicans swooped along the rollers, dragging their feet
only inches above the water. Burt felt a curious mixture
of dread and euphoria; such peace was too delicious to
last.

He left the water, showered, shaved, walked to the
club and downed three rum punches while waiting for
Joss to wake up from her afternoon nap and start her
customary evening drinking. The sun sank into a rosy
haze, and darkness came down like a purple curtain.
Godfrey set a table for two and suspended a Coleman
lantern from a beam. Joss appeared at last, and Burt
saw why she'd been delayed. She'd put on a dress,
something she usually wore only for trips to St. Vincent
or further. Rarer still, she wore a necklace and earrings, and a scent of violets had replaced her usual aura
of saltwater, fish and rum.

They ate langouste tail by candlelight and washed it
down with French wine. Joss talked with sparkling gai-
ety, and for a time Burt was in love with her. The
white light of the Coleman lantern glowed on her bare
shoulders and descended into the valley of her bosom;
the surf thumped and rumbled; the breeze carried the
smell of the sea into the club. Burt felt primitive and
extremely male. It occurred to him that Joss had been
without a husband for nearly a year, and that he himself was now free of ties. The pounding sea ringed the
island and made it a private world.

He looked up as Godfrey shuffled out of the night
carrying an empty tray. "Mrs. Keener's?"

Joss answered with a trace of sarcasm, "Your lady friend is too delicate to eat in the presence of others."

Burt smiled. "You'd rather she joined us?"

"Hell, I don't care." She waved her hand impatiently. "No, that's wrong. I'd just as soon leave her alone. Her husband's letter mentioned a nervous breakdown, said his wife needed rest and quiet and no disturbance." She frowned. "He said he'd been here before, but I can't remember." She leaned forward confidentially. "I'll tell you a secret, Burt. I don't remember people. A week after they leave they get lost in a sea of faces. People think it's my poor eyesight when I don't recognize them again. I let 'em think it. One of the tricks of the trade."

Joss started on rum, and soon her cheeks were flushed and her voice low and husky. Burt drank with her, more than he should, in an attempt to recapture his earlier romantic glow. But it only saddened him. Finally, Joss put her warm hand on his knee.

"Burt, there's something you learn on an island, to accept your own nature. Don't worry about the boy you shot."

Burt felt himself tense. "What's that got to do with my nature?"

"You're a cop, you did your job—"

"Maybe that's the problem."

"Burt, if you weren't a cop you'd be on the other side. You've got a violent nature. It shows in your eyes, like smoke behind a window. You're a rough, hard man—"

"A killer, the newspapers said."

She pushed away her glass. "Oh, hell, I goofed. I wanted to cheer you up, but I got you mad."

"I'm not mad."

"Don't kid me, Burt. You talk soft and you move slow, but it shows. Your body changes. You turn into sharp edges and brutal bone. I had a boy friend once—" She stopped and drew a deep breath. She got up suddenly, and stood swaying, her eyes bright. She spoke in a husky voice: "I'm stoned, Burt. Take me up to bed."

He helped her up the crumbling stone steps behind the beach club and into her one-room cabin. She sat heavily on the bed. "Don't light the lamp, Burt."

"No."

He walked silently to the door. Behind him came the faint rustle and snap of clothing.

"Come here, Burt, and help me with this damn hook."

"No, Joss," he said, opening the door. "I don't think we will."

He was groping his way down the steps when he heard her voice behind him. "Burt, where are you going?"

"Good night, Joss."

The door slammed, hard, and Burt smiled to himself. Joss would have only a vague recollection tomorrow, just enough to look at him uneasily and wonder exactly what she'd said and done. Maybe she'd eliminate him as a candidate for husband number seven or eight, whichever it was.

His head felt light. Not so straight yourself, March. Better take a walk, sober up, avoid tomorrow's hangover. He left the path and walked between cabins three and four to the beach. He walked on the sand and let the spray blow in his face. The surf thundered; the fumaroles moaned. He decided to put on his trunks and take a swim. As he passed cabin two, he saw the yellow glow of lamplight in the window. Strange woman, up late and alone . . .

There was a warning as he opened his cabin door— perhaps a pressure in the air, a smell, or a mental message. Someone else was in the room. He whirled, wasting a precious second in reaching for his absent shoulder holster. Something struck his right shoulder so hard it numbed his arm and sent pain shooting to his fingertips. Burt had no idea who his attacker might be; he didn't even think about it. Here was hostility, and questions would have to wait. He swung his fist at a shadowy bulk and struck a glancing blow somewhere high on the face. There was a sound strangely like a laugh. Could it be? Burt saw the pale blob of a face, and a vivid whiteness where the mouth should be. Lord, he *was* smiling, white teeth flashing. Burt swung again, discovered too late that he'd put his weight on his bad leg. *Fool . . . too much booze.* He missed, staggered forward, and clutched at the other man. The man moved back, quick as a cat, and Burt realized he was going to fall. He didn't feel himself hit the floor; something struck the back of his neck and all the light went out of his mind.

TWO

Joss's voice sliced through a shrieking whistle in his brain.

"You've made a mistake, Mr. Keener, this is a guest, Burt March."

"Yes?" said a calm, cultured male voice. "What was he doing in my cabin?"

"He . . . I said he could use it. Until you came."

Her voice seemed to come from a great distance, but Burt could tell she was still muddled from drink. Slowly he extended his senses; he smelled Joss's perfume, felt a soft fabric beneath his neck. Under that was firm flesh. He opened one eye a slit and saw that he lay on the floor with his head across Joss's thighs. Looking up beyond the curving shelf of her bosom (she wore the robe he'd given her; beneath that there seemed to be only Joss) Burt saw the faintly pouched underside of her chin. Without moving his head he traced her gaze to a man seated on the bed. His legs were crossed negligently, and he was cleaning his nails with a penknife. In the glow of the kerosene lamp, the man looked very tall, with wax-blond hair, blue eyes, and a neat blond mustache. He could have been made up for a part in a Hollywood yachting movie; blue jacket, white linen scarf, white trousers, and white canvas shoes. Burt saw a reddened swelling high on his cheek; it looked incongruous on the porcelain serenity of the face, like a wart on a Dresden doll.

Burt groaned and sat up, blinking his eyes. "What happened?"

"Burt! I was telling Mr. Keener—"

"I'll explain," said the man, and without halting his nail-cleaning operation, regarding his hands from time to time in the lamplight, he introduced himself as Rolf Keener. He'd rented a power-launch in St. Vincent and piloted himself to the island. The surf must have covered the sound of his arrival, since nobody had met him at the jetty. However, since he remembered the island from his last visit, he'd gone directly to his own cabin. He'd just arrived when he heard a prowler outside. Nervous in a strange land, he'd waited behind the door. When the prowler attacked, he'd simply defended himself.

"You swung first," said Burt, aware of a throbbing pain in the back of his neck.

"That may be true." Keener smiled. "I was frightened, you understand."

Yeah, thought Burt, you looked scared with that smile on your face. Keener told a logical story—within the limits of his own logic. If Keener hadn't stopped to see his wife, then she couldn't have told him about the man in cabin one. But why hadn't he stopped to see her? And it was possible that he'd failed to see Burt's suitcase under the bed, or his wet swim trunks on the porch railing, since he hadn't lit a lamp. But if a man is so scared that he attacks the first man who enters, why would he himself enter a strange cabin without a light? There was something wrong here. . . .

Keener rose from the bed and walked to the door. "I'll sleep in my wife's cabin tonight; tomorrow we can make other arrangements." He turned on a smile which did nothing but display perfect white teeth. "You were rather lucky, March. Trespassers are often shot."

Burt stood up and walked toward Keener. He felt tight, ready. "That has a sound I don't like, Keener. If there's anything left to settle, let's do it now."

For a second their eyes locked. Burt glimpsed something hooded and watchful in the other's eyes; maybe it was only his imagination, but there seemed to be a small wizened creature with gray leathery wings, folded and waiting, behind the smooth face. Then Rolf Keener smiled.

"Let's forget it, March." Half-ruefully, he touched

the bump on his cheek. "We've drawn each other's blood. That means we can dispense with a lot of needless formality. Why not step next door for a drink?"

"No, thanks," said Burt. "I seem to have acquired a headache."

Rolf Keener chuckled and walked away. Burt walked through the door and watched him disappear around the banyan; he moved quickly and surely, like a night-hunting animal.

As Burt started back to his cabin, he saw the half-moon sinking down through a pale mist in the west. With a shock he realized that it must be nearly three A.M. It couldn't have been past eleven when he'd left Joss—

The screen door opened softly behind him. Burt jumped, then saw it was Joss, clutching her robe together at the neck.

"Joss, what time did Keener come up and get you?"

"He . . . didn't." She bit her lip. "I came down to see you."

"Why?"

"I don't know. I guess, to finish the mess I started, really botch it up good." She shrugged. "I was still drunk. I'm sober now. When I came in and saw you lying on the floor—"

"Where was Rolf?"

"Sitting on the bed. Said he was waiting for you to wake up so he could ask why you'd broken in."

"Four hours, just sitting there?"

"I guess." She frowned up at him. "You sound suspicious."

"Suspicion is an occupational hazard, Joss. But there's something damn strange about both those people. You may have drawn a couple of nuts."

"Oh, well, aren't we all? I was lying on my hammock a week ago and my first husband came walking up. Wearing hip boots and carrying a fishpole. He asked me if it was a good day for surf-casting and I said sure. He started walking to the beach and disappeared. Next day I decided I was going nuts."

"Not that way, Joss. This guy ... if the way he jumped me is any sign, has a more dangerous problem. It's called paranoia."

"I've never tried it."

"Don't, Joss. You can't enjoy it like you enjoy your everyday run-of-the-mill hallucinations. And it's so logical it's hard to see through it. If a man's trying to kill you, and you're sure of it, you'd probably try to get him first. Right? Sure, that's logical. Or call the cops. Well, a paranoiac works the same way. The only thing is, nobody's trying to kill him. It's all delusion. He tells the cops and they say sure and do nothing. So the nut decides everybody's against him, the cops, the whole world. A guy reaches in his pocket for a cigarette, blam! The nut shoots, figuring he was going for a gun. I remember a case, a man was cutting a roast at Sunday dinner, then suddenly he turned and stabbed his wife in the stomach. She'd poisoned the meat, he said. Another guy shot a man because he bumped into his car. Later he told the cops the other guy had done it in order to hold him there until help arrived. They were all plotting to kill him—"

"Oh, Burt. Mr. Keener was so calm, relaxed—"

"Yes. And wasn't that strange, under the circumstances?"

"Maybe. I'm not sure what you mean."

"Well, I didn't think he was really relaxed. He could have been wound up so tight that he didn't dare allow a single emotion to disturb the surface. That's another mark of the psychopath, Joss; he's so torn up inside that he can't let his mask slip for fear the whole thing will collapse."

"Burt ..." She shivered and drew her robe tighter. "You're giving me the creeps. I'll give back their money and tell 'em to leave."

"No, I'm only guessing. I think I'll have another look at him, right now. He did invite me for a drink."

"What'll I do?"

"Go to bed. I'll see you tomorrow."

The lamp was lit on the veranda of cabin two, and

Rolf Keener was seated at the hand-hewn wooden table with a glass before him. When Burt tapped on the door, Rolf waved at a glass on the other side of the table. "Come in. There's yours."

Dazed, Burt walked in and sat down. "I said I wasn't coming. Why did you expect me?"

"Because you are what you are, Sergeant."

A physical shock tingled along Burt's nerves. His mind whirled for an instant, then he remembered he'd been out four hours. "You went through my things."

Rolf shrugged. "I checked your identification. Wouldn't you have done the same to me?"

Thoughtfully, Burt had to admit to himself that it was true. "It isn't the same thing—"

"Why not? Are you on duty now? Do you carry any warrants?"

Burt frowned at Keener. The subject of his status had been dragged into the conversation by the scruff of the neck; Burt wondered why the man had been so eager for that piece of information.

"I'm not on duty, Keener. But if you found out I was a cop, why the big act with Joss?"

Rolf nodded. "You're good. Very sharp. I put on that act because ..." He shrugged. "I like to keep as many people as ignorant as possible."

"But you let me know. You didn't have to."

Rolf closed his eyes a minute, then opened them. "That confuses things even more, doesn't it?"

He gave a hollow laugh which sent a prickle of dread up Burt's spine. Here was a man not entirely in control of himself; a man who could work himself into a corner where he'd have to shoot his way out. You never knew what would seem a reason for killing, to a man like that, and Burt began to feel jumpy. He couldn't remember ever having been afraid of a man before, but Rolf came close to filling the bill.

Something else. The silence between their words was filled with the rustle of a mattress, the scrape of sandals on concrete, the crackle of a match. Burt smelled cigarette smoke through the closed door. Mrs. Keener was awake and attentive, but apparently he still wasn't to see the woman of mystery.

"Tell me about the detective business," said Rolf abruptly.

"Tell me about your business."

Rolf smiled. "I'm an importer. Very interesting the way I got into it. I don't suppose you were in World War II . . ."

"I was a kid," said Burt. "I sold war stamps and collected paper."

"Yes," the man smiled benignly. "Well, I was in the Office of Strategic Services, the OSS. I happen to be of European extraction, I suppose you detect the accent."

"No."

"No? Well, it's been a long time. In the OSS I commanded a group which went into occupied countries to organize partisan groups. We sometimes used the local currency, but usually we carried a more negotiable commodity, gold, jewels, that sort of thing. To buy guns, food, and allies. It was often necessary to kill men, you understand—"

"It goes without saying in wartime," said Burt. "Why say it?"

"Because . . . I have a point to make." He leaned forward, his eyes bright. "Every man has a killer inside him, March. With some people it's weak and easy to hold down. With others it's strong; you try to hold it down and you can feel it snarling and growling inside you." He leaned back and smiled. "I call it the beast."

"I see," said Burt.

"I'm sure you do."

The words came as a shock, and Burt wondered if the other had read his thoughts. For the talk of war spun Burt back to Korea, to those long nights on the parallel when one patrol had followed another, night after night, until death and danger had become a part of life like eating and sleeping, and almost as necessary. One night he'd gone out alone and come back with his knife bloody, and all he would remember afterwards was that a Chinese loudspeaker had played *Sentimental Journey.*

"Go on, Rolf," said Burt in a tight voice. "You were telling about World War II."

"Yes. I let my beast out in those days. I let him rage and snarl and gorge himself; I was a hero, a patriot, but I was never foolish enough to think that society would let the beast run loose when there was no longer any need for him. So after the war I threw the chains on him."

"Did you?"

"Ah, you're thinking about our fight." Rolf reached for the bottle and poured a drink, thoughtfully watching the liquor rise in the glass. He proffered the bottle to Burt, but Burt shook his head, waiting. Rolf capped the bottle, then raised his glass and smiled. "Well, March, you have to feed the beast from time to time. Someday you may need him to save your life."

He leaned back and drank, closing his eyes as though the liquor were a delicious elixir. "Ah well, so I chained up the beast and searched for a socially acceptable occupation. I'd seen millions of dollars' worth of war materials all over the world; now it would never be used. Mile-long rows of airplanes, tanks, jeeps, command cars, rusting on islands, in deserts, mountains. Why not remove the smaller units, radios, optical instruments, electronic gear, ship it home and sell it? You may know how that turned out; the men with government contacts and money covered the deal like a blanket. I made a few thousand, the others made millions before the stink reached the public. Then I thought of Europe, fugitive Nazis with their little caches of jewelry, gold, and art objects. I had the cash, and contacts who could provide them with new identities, and a safe hiding place—"

"You helped Nazis?"

"I'm a businessman, not a patriot. Others took their money and denounced them to the authorities, but I fulfilled my contracts. Is that unethical?"

Burt shrugged; he couldn't get rid of his distaste for

Rolf. The man was likable enough; handsome, worldly and friendly. That was it. He was a good deal more friendly than the situation warranted.

But Rolf was telling how fugitive Nazis had led him to South America. There he'd seen an untapped reservoir of wealth in Indian artifacts; gold, silver, jewelry, pottery, and objects of art. For several years he'd moved the stuff out by bribery and smuggling, selling it to private collectors and museums in the States. But there'd been no limit to the money-hunger of South American *politicos;* the overhead had risen and finally wiped out his profit margin. So he'd liquidated the business and was now at liberty, so to speak, looking for new opportunities.

And he needs a cop, thought Burt. Here it comes.

Instead Rolf said, "Your turn now, March."

Burt realized that the effort of trying to stay ahead of Rolf Keener had amplified his headache into a throbbing agony.

"I'll have to save my story. This headache—"

"My wife can cure that. Ah . . . Tracy?"

Burt turned, half-expecting to see Mrs. Keener in her usual all-concealing attire. But she came out the door bareheaded, and in the pale yellow light of the kerosene lamp her face shone faintly with skin-cream. Her nose was short and faintly tilted on the end. Black hair billowed around her shoulders. He tried to see her eyes, but they were squinted as though she'd come out of total darkness. Her beach coat reached only to mid-thigh and somehow suggested that there was nothing beneath it. That was an unwarranted conclusion, Burt decided; something about the island kept a man on the edge of criminal assault.

"Tracy, can you give Burt March one of your headache treatments?"

"Of course." She smiled a polite smile that held no warmth. There was a poised smoothness about the way she walked toward him; the studied glide of a model in a high fashion show. He tightened up as she walked behind him, then he was enclosed in the aura of her perfume, and her cool fingers began drawing the pain from the back of his neck.

Rolf looked on with the benevolent manner of a father. "She told me how she cooled you this afternoon after you returned her purse. Then I gave you the business in your cabin. You've been treated badly by the Keener family, and we'd like to make it up."

The words made Burt feel prickly, uncomfortable. He leaned forward, away from the woman. "This isn't necessary. I've got aspirin."

"Let her," said Rolf. "She doesn't mind, do you, Tracy?"

"Of course not," said the voice behind him. Her warm breath caressed his neck.

How do you deal with this friendliness, wondered Burt, particularly when you don't think it's real? The whole scene had the unreality of a poorly acted but carefully rehearsed play. The lines were perfect, but there were those very small split-second errors in timing. Rolf, particularly, had the manner of a man reading a script; sometimes he forgot to smile, sometimes he remembered at the wrong time . . .

All right, Burt decided. Play along. You don't learn if you don't listen. He leaned back and let the fingers continue their work. She had achieved an even rhythm which Burt found vaguely sexual. It was difficult to keep from sighing with pleasure. How could a man sit there and let his wife do that to another man?

Wind ripped through the palm trees. The surf thundered; the house trembled. The fumaroles moaned.

"Tide going out," said Burt.

Rolf stood up. "I'll see to the launch. Don't leave."

And Burt sat, aware that there must be method in Rolf's madness of leaving him alone with his wife. Better relax and see what kind of approach she used.

She didn't keep him waiting long. The screen door had scarcely closed when her treatment ceased to be therapy and became a caress. Her fingertips tingled along his jaw, up behind his ears. She blew softly on his neck.

Burt jumped, and she laughed. "Are you one of those men who let a woman do it all?"

The fact that he'd half-expected it didn't dull the surprise of hearing it spoken. She was, if not making a proposition, unmistakably inviting one. What the hell did this island do to women, anyway?

"I was wondering," said Burt, "if you found everything intact in your purse."

"Certainly," she said in a disinterested voice. Then, curiously: "What has that to do with it?"

Burt shrugged. Of course she wouldn't mention the heroin, and he'd better drop the subject before she suspected that he knew. Strange that the woman showed none of the drug's stigmata; still, it was hard to pick a well-fed hypo out of a crowd, unless she happened to be on the nod or badly strung out . . .

"You understand about this afternoon," she said, leaning forward in a way that brought a soft double-pressure against his back. "I wanted to invite you in for a drink, but I knew he was coming. I didn't want him to find—"

Burt laughed.

"What's funny?"

"I've seen women who come on strong when their husbands are near, then turn cold when it's safe."

"Oh?" Idly, her fingers stirred the hair at the back of his head. "You think I'm one of those?"

"I think you enjoy the game, yes. I could die of old age waiting for the pay-off."

"Tell you what you do, Sergeant March. You know the island. You name it. Time, place, everything. I'll meet you."

Burt stopped laughing. "I think you're trying to set me up, Mrs. Keener. Don't."

She was leaning on him, her chin gently gouging his shoulder. Her breath was warm in his ear. "What are you afraid of, Sergeant March? I thought cops weren't afraid of anyone."

"That's enough. I'm leaving." Burt started to get up, but her arms slid around his neck and pulled him back.

The soft breath against his ear became wetness, then sharp, biting pain. He twisted and overturned the chair. He fell and felt her soft form rolling beneath him. He struggled to his feet and put his hand to his ear. Warm blood trickled down his neck. He felt foolish and resentful, as though he'd been tricked into performing in a slapstick comedy.

"Damn!" Burt looked down at the woman. Her beach robe was in drastic disarray, but she didn't seem to notice. She was laughing, and there was a bright red wetness on her lower lip.

"You need a good beating," he told her.

"Really?" She sat up with her arms braced behind her, stretching her long muscular legs out on the concrete floor. "Go ahead, Sergeant. Do your duty."

"Oh hell—!" He whirled and tore open the screen door. Behind him her laughter trilled high above the sound of the surf. As he walked back to his cabin, he realized this was almost the same scene he'd walked out on earlier. Except that Joss had no ulterior motives; or if she had, they were hidden even from Joss herself. Mrs. Keener had a sick thing going, and Burt had a feeling her husband was a part of it.

He took a shower before going to bed. It helped a little.

THREE

Next morning Burt found a shining new padlock on the door of cabin two. He shoved his hands into his pockets and regarded it with a feeling of frustration; he had merely glanced toward the cabin as he walked along the beach, feeling normal curiosity, and now ... now he felt an aching desire to go in. The detective syndrome, he thought; you see a locked door and you want to look behind it. Or is that a burglar syndrome? Maybe there wasn't much difference.

He walked toward the club. It was a gray day, and a steady east wind carried moisture in such fine particles that he didn't know it was raining until he found his hair damp. The lagoon was like a blanket being shaken; the surf washed over the jetty and made tentative passes at the pilings which held up the beach club. Rolf's launch was gone, and Burt could hear Joss's voice raised in shrill anger behind the kitchen.

He found her standing over Coco, who was squatting on the ground, sullenly picking a scab on his instep.

"What's wrong?" asked Burt.

Joss turned, looking sheepish. "This ignorant ass let the rowboat drift away last night."

Coco looked up. "Mist' March, I leave it on the beach where the surf do not reach."

"Let's go see."

In front, Coco showed him the boat's keel mark in the sand. It extended three feet above the line of coral, driftwood and coconut husks which marked the high-water point.

"She lie here when I go to sleep," said Coco. "Not here this morning."

"You must have moved it," said Joss.

43

"No, mistress. I am sure."

They all stood looking at the marks in the sand as though, if they looked long enough, the boat would materialize. Finally Coco shuffled off, mumbling. Joss shrugged. "Weather like this bugs these people. They don't know it, but it does."

Burt walked with her to the club. "What bugs me is losing the boat."

Joss waved her hand airily and sat down at a table. "Hell, it wasn't worth much. It's just that one by one all my rowboats disappear. That boy gets out there day-dreaming and a boat gets carried onto the rocks; he forgets to put in a drainplug and a boat swamps; he goes skin-diving alone and his boat drifts away." She sighed and signaled Godfrey to bring coffee. "I'll get another one made on Bequia. Meanwhile there's no problem. I just bought a pile of supplies, food and liquor, with the money I got from Keener and Smith. And O'Ryan will be through again in two or three days."

"Suppose somebody gets sick?"

"You feeling bad?" She eyed him quizzically, then shrugged. "I'm sure, if there was an emergency, Rolf Keener would lend his launch."

At that point Burt realized what really bothered him about losing the rowboat. Rolf Keener now had the only means of transportation on the island—and Rolf Keener had gone out early this morning to check his launch.

"Where'd the Keeners go?" he asked.

"For a cruise," said Joss.

Burt frowned at the frothing sea. Fifteen-foot rollers broke against the rocks around the lagoon and sent up explosions of spray. Black-toothed rocks bit through the surface each time a wave receded.

"He's in no danger, Burt," said Joss. "He's got twin outboards, besides his inboard engine, and he seemed to know what he was doing."

"Yes," said Burt. "He gives that impression."

Godfrey brought two mugs of French coffee, hot and

strong and heavy with chicory. Burt sipped it slowly, squinting out beyond the dripping thatch. He thought about Rolf, not because he feared for his safety, but because he wondered what could lure a man out to sea in this weather.

"You made a good impression on him," said Joss after a long silence. "He said you could keep cabin one. He wants you for a neighbor."

Burt gave a wry smile. "I wonder what else he wants."

"Why?"

"He told me his life story last night. Some men do it because they like to talk. Rolf isn't a compulsive talker. I think he wanted to exchange confidences."

"Did you?"

"Wasn't much more I could tell. He knew I was with the police, searched my wallet while I was out cold."

Her mouth dropped open. "No! But that doesn't sound like—"

She broke off as Jata appeared at the railing and morosely held up a mop and a bucket. "Miss Joss, how I'm cleaning cabin two?"

"You'll have to wait, Jata. Mr. Keener wants to be there when you clean."

The old woman's blue-black, wrinkled face settled slowly into a mask of fury. She turned and strode off, somehow managing to convey injured dignity in the way she planted her large bare feet on the sand. Burt regarded Joss with a question in his eyes, and Joss looked down into her coffee. She spoke defensively:

"It sounded perfectly reasonable when he explained it this morning. I ... didn't realize how it would sound."

"Yes. He's very logical ... in his own way." Burt frowned. "I wonder what valuables he had that he couldn't take with him."

Joss wasn't listening. She gulped down her coffee and stood up. "I'd better go soothe Jata's pride. See you at lunch."

Burt breakfasted on soursop juice, fried breadfruit

and red snapper. Boris was sorry, but the rats had stolen the eggs and the mongooses had eaten all the chickens and there was no way to get off the island until
Mister Keener returned.

Burt felt a new twist of unease. "If he weren't here
how would you get off?"

"We would cut the glass, sir."

"Cut the glass?"

"Take the mirror, go up to the *piton,* catch the sun
and flash it to the fishing boats."

"And if there's no sun?"

"If there is no sun, then you wait. The sun always
return."

After breakfast, Burt climbed the steep stony path
which had been hacked through the shoulder-high
grass. By the time he reached the base of the three
black crags, he had to stop and massage his aching leg.
Maybe I'm pushing too hard, he thought, can't afford
to get crippled up at this point.

At what point? Well, before it happens, whatever
Rolf is going to make happen. . . .

A six-foot watchtower had been built on the highest
crag, dating from the days when the French and En-
glish had been killing each other to plant their flags
around the world. The eminence was a paved area no
larger than a shot-put ring, with a waist-high parapet
halfway around it. The rest of the parapet had fallen a
breath-taking five hundred feet to the rocks below. Burt
leaned his elbows on the parapet, breathing heavily as
he scanned the horizon. The mist-laden wind cooled his
flushed face. Clots of low gray clouds floated over the
white-capped sea below, seemingly anchored by silver
streamers of rain. To the north, the populus island of
Bequia formed an irregular crescent, pointing a gnarled
finger at the southern tip of St. Vincent. To the south,
a score of smaller islands thrust up from the sea, some
so close together that it was hard to see where one began and another ended. He had visited all of them in
the past; he recognized the jutting red peak of Bat-
towia, inhabited by a few native farmers; he saw the

wooded, rolling hills of Cannouan, the twisting spine of Baliceaux, the yellow-green pastures of Mustique, and the jagged thousand-foot spires of Union. Most of the smaller islands were waterless and uninhabited except for semiwild sheep and cattle, and voracious sandflies. There were none of the usual fishing boats bobbing between the islands, and no sign of Rolf's power cruiser.

He left the tower and strolled aimlessly around the island. At least, he thought he was strolling aimlessly; he realized his subconscious had taken charge when he found himself regarding once again the padlock on cabin two. There was nobody in sight. He walked around the cabin looking for a means of ingress. The windows were small and hooked on the inside. The padlock hung on a rusty hasp screwed into rotting wood; he could have ripped it loose but he wanted to leave no sign.

He stumbled over an accumulation of litter from the cabin: broken bottles, rusty cans, and charred newspapers, all damp and glistening. One small pile had not yet been burned; he supposed it included Mrs. Keener's sweepings. He got a stick and poked through it. Several wads of lipsticked tissue. Funny, there were two different shades, one the dark red he'd seen in the purse, the other a pale orange. Mmm. Maybe women changed their lipstick according to mood. Here was a mass of tangled, knotted hair, filled with lint as though it had been cleaned from a comb. He pulled an end loose and examined it. A pale wavy hair, ash blonde. Not Rolf Keener's, too long for that. Possibly from a woman guest who predated Mrs. Keener, fallen in a corner and swept out only recently. Have to ask Joss. He looked for something to keep the hair in. All the paper was charred and soggy; ah, here was one, wadded up into a tight little ball like a piece of popcorn. He smoothed it and found that there were two sheets of thin airmail stationery. It had been burned carelessly, and much of the writing remained legible. The salutation caught his eye:

r Rolf,
                    Three nights on this island
           away from you have given me a
                               nk about all that has
                         ce I married you and

So, it was written by Mrs. Keener in a blunt vertical
script totally without flourishes. He had not expected
her to write in such a near-masculine hand. He spread
out the second sheet and found only one and a half
sentences intact:

                    no point in going on
           dreading every tomorrow and regretting each

A coldness grew at the back of his neck. He'd read
many suicide notes, and this had the ring of authentic-
ity. Funny, he thought, folding the letter and shoving it
into the pocket of his shorts; this was written by a quietly desperate woman who had decided to end her marriage, perhaps even her life. He couldn't picture Mrs.
Keener in that part at all.

Well, that settled one thing. He had to get inside. He
circled the cabin again and saw that the bathroom was
roofed with corrugated tin. Probably it had once been
thatched, but moisture had rotted the grass. A ladder
led up to a platform which held a barrel of water for
the shower. Burt climbed up and found that the roofing
had merely been laid in place and covered with heavy
stones to keep it from blowing away. He moved the
stones, propped the sheeting open with a stick, and
crawled inside. Standing on the low stand which held
the basin, he pulled out the stick and lowered the roof
back in place.

Inside, he noticed that Mrs. Keener had the same
habit of untidiness he'd found in many otherwise at-
tractive women. Her robe hung on the bathroom door
and a pair of black panties were draped over the
shower head. He touched his fingers to the transparent,
chiffon-like fabric. Little red lips were embroidered

around the bottom. It was the kind of lingerie teen-agers order from the little ads at the backs of true con-fession magazines.

And what did that prove about Mrs. Keener? Simply that she took pride in her sexuality and liked to adorn it as well as possible. All of which fit the woman he had—met was too weak a word: encountered, maybe, or engaged. Such a woman would hardly consider suicide; if she did, she would write a fiery renunciation of the world, then reconsider and seek renewed life in an affair with a new man.

He froze at the entrance to the bedroom. Had a win-dow blown open or . . . what was that breath of cold-ness? All the windows were closed. Burt didn't have Joss's blind faith in the supernatural, but he'd run into things which couldn't be explained any other way. There was a feeling which often came to him in a scent of past violence; it had been present in the jewelry store, it was here now. A residue of fear or pain, like an invisible mist weighting the air.

He shook off the feeling and made a quick, thorough search of the room. More feminine clothing and inex-pensive jewelry—in rather garish taste, he thought—but only one overnight case which held male clothing. Inside the case was a box of thirty-eight caliber ammu-nition. He catalogued the fact without emotion; Rolf had a gun, no doubt he kept it on the boat. A paranoiac with a gun was a combination devoutly to be avoided under any circumstances, but he had no time to consider it now.

He found the olive-green purse, but the talcum pow-der and the wallet were gone. Curious; it was as though Rolf had known his cabin would be searched. After re-moving all traces of incriminating evidence, why had he padlocked the door? Because he knew that would tit-illate Burt's curiosity? Damn, he didn't like the feeling of being always one step behind the man. . . .

He jumped at the sound of tapping on glass. "Sir! Sir!" He saw Maudie's round face pressed against the window. "They comin back, sir."

He hurriedly glanced around the room, satisfied himself that he'd left no signs of his search, and departed the way he had come. Maudie was waiting as he dropped to the ground. He saw no point in asking how she'd known he was in the cabin; she'd been following him, of course. Didn't she always?

He walked away from the cabin and stopped beneath the palm trees. "You know what I was doing in there?"

"No, sir. I think, yes."

He frowned, trying to decipher her patois. "You don't know, but you have an idea?"

She nodded. "I think you place charm to kill him. Because he bash you."

He looked at her and smiled slowly. "You've lived with your mother too long."

"Yes, sir."

She seemed to be waiting for something more, and Burt reddened at the realization that his words could be taken as some sort of proposal. Maudie wore his gift beneath her T-shirt, and it was, as he'd expected, far too small. He failed to see how she breathed. He thought of telling her she didn't have to wear it to please him, then realized it would merely drag him into more semantic confusion. He shrugged and started toward the club. Maudie followed. Burt called over his shoulder:

"Keep following me around, Maudie, and you'll see things you shouldn't."

"Yes, sir," she said gravely.

He walked on, and heard her bare feet slapping the path behind him.

He reached the club in time to watch Rolf negotiate the entrance to the lagoon. A split-second's error in timing would have ripped the bottom out of the sleek, lap-hulled Swedish cruiser, but whatever else Rolf was, he was a skilled boatman. He waited for the swell, then gunned the engine and rose up with it. A wall of spray hid the boat for a moment, then it sailed into the comparatively calm lagoon. Burt was waiting as Rolf tied up at the jetty.

"We've lost our rowboat," said Burt. "You didn't happen to see it drifting?"

Rolf stood up, three inches taller than Burt. He looked strikingly virile and Nordic with his yellow hair blowing and his windbreaker jacket sparkling with water droplets. Burt noted the bulge beneath his left armpit and was half-relieved to know where the gun was.

The woman stood behind him, her eyes hidden by dark glasses. Her nose and forehead were sunburned, and there was pinkness on the long legs which extended below her white shorts. He wondered at her folly in submitting herself to the sun after being burned yesterday. Perhaps she'd been deceived by the haze; many northerners didn't realize the tropic sun could burn through a layer of clouds.

"There was nothing out there," said Rolf. "Everybody seems to be staying in port." He frowned. "Lost the rowboat, eh?" His eyelids drooped slightly. "Then it seems I'm in possession of the only means of leaving the island." He smiled blandly at Burt. "Let me know if I can be of any help."

He walked away, and the woman followed without having spoken, or even nodded to Burt. He noticed that the shorts molded her so snugly that the cloth was shiny tight. It seemed wrong for her to be so blatantly sexual in public; she was the type who waited until it could produce immediate results. Furthermore, she wasn't handling herself in a seductive manner. She walked as though she were self-conscious and uncomfortable, as though she'd been caught unprepared and had to wear a smaller woman's clothing—

"All right, March. Shove your eyes back in your head."

He turned to Joss beside him. "You notice anything strange about Mrs. Keener?"

"It isn't strange. Everybody's got one. Not everybody throws it around."

He had to smile at Joss's criticism of another woman's apparel, considering her own home-made bathing costume. He walked with her to the club and sat down at a table.

"Tell me, did a blonde happen to occupy cabin two before she came?"

Joss frowned. "No. The last ones were two Frenchmen from Martinique. Rum-heads. Threw up all over the joint. Had to scrub it with soap and water to get the smell out. Why?"

"When did Jata clean it last?"

"Yesterday. She couldn't today because—"

"I know. Then it had to be night before last."

"What?"

He hesitated, then pulled out the two sheets of paper and handed them to her. She squinted, then shook her head and handed them back. "Light's bad here. You read."

"The light's perfect and you know it." Burt read the two notes and explained where he'd found them. He didn't mention that he'd gone inside.

"Okay, Burt," said Joss without interest. "She was alone and bugged by the fact."

"Bugged enough to consider suicide?"

"Enough to write a note about it, and enjoy the thought of her husband being sorry she was dead. It's like a crying drunk; you feel way down, you can't figure why you're down, so you invent trouble."

"Maybe." Burt folded the sheets and returned them to his pocket. "But you've got to admit, she doesn't seem to be feeling sorry for herself now."

"So her husband came and she's happy." Joss raised her glass, obviously ready to forget Mrs. Keener.

"One more thing," said Burt. "Have you noticed any changes in her since I came? Has she dyed her hair . . . or anything?"

She set down her glass. "Burt, she had only one head, she wore clothes, she didn't wear a beard. That's all I can tell you. You know my eyesight."

"Maybe the boys—"

"They won't tell you anything."

Her positive tone made Burt look at her sharply.
"Why not?"

"Well . . . they're not supposed to look." Joss looked
uncomfortable. "We've had some trouble in the past.
The boys are typical islanders, you know, pretty direct
types. Uninhibited. When they see a pretty woman they
. . . look her over. But good. Stateside women aren't
used to that, and most of them have this color thing. I
finally had to give strict orders to the boys, don't look
at the women."

"Hell, Joss. That won't stop it."

"No, but they still won't tell you anything. That
would mean admitting they've disobeyed."

Burt had to agree, and reflected that here was the
drawback in throwing your authority around; you cut
yourself off from sources of information. He decided
not to tell Joss about the heroin, nor about the suspicion which was taking shape in his mind. Joss couldn't
help him until he knew which way it was going, and
there was no point in spreading the burden of silence.
With Joss, it would be a tremendous burden. He supposed it was her stage background that made her accept people for what they said they were. It was part of
her charm.

Joss broke into his thoughts with somber sincerity:

"Listen, Burt, I don't know what that bump on the
head did to you, but you're going to louse up your holiday. Not only that, you'll depress me, and then I'll
drink too much and go on a bawling jag—"

"I'm sorry, Joss, but—"

"But, nothing. The weather's bad enough without
you catfooting around the island. What we need is a
party."

It occurred to Burt that a party might be exactly
what he needed to shake out more information.
"You're right, Joss. Get the boys in with their instruments—"

"And I'll broil pigeons, and get some more wine—"
She paused. "The Keeners?"

"Invite them, by all means. It won't be a party if
they don't come."

FOUR

Joss managed to produce excellent wine for the dinner, and pigeons braised over the charcoals. She also arranged that Burt set opposite Mrs. Keener, with Rolf opposite Joss. Burt could see her visibly melting under the man's attention, hypnotically reaching for her glass when Keener filled it.

Burt devoted his attention to Mrs. Keener, and in the process grew increasingly puzzled. She seemed miserably ill at ease in a dress too small for her. Its décolletage might have been breathtaking had her cleavage not been so grotesquely distorted. Burt half-expected to hear a pop like a champagne cork coming out of a bottle, and to see Mrs. Keener shoot up to the roof. She kept squirming in her chair, plucking at her waist, and plunging a hand inside her dress to make certain adjustments when she thought Burt wasn't watching. Though she ate only one pigeon, she seldom raised her eyes from her plate. When she did, Burt saw the sparkle of moisture inside her lids. He felt a rising excitement; watery eyes, loss of appetite, itching, all were signs of drug withdrawal. But if she really were an addict, that blew his whole theory to hell. Then he remembered something which restored it; he had delivered fourteen caps to her, and there would have been no reason for her to be deprived.

When he tried to engage her in conversation, she answered in monosyllables without looking up. Each time she spoke, Rolf would pause in his talk with Joss, stiffen, and relax only when she finished. Finally Burt asked:

"Where did you work, Mrs. Keener, before you were married?"

55

Nobody moved, but Burt could feel the air stretch taut like a balloon about to burst. Rolf pushed back his plate and asked with a half-smile:

"Tell me something, Burt. How does it feel to arrest a man?"

Joss looked annoyed at this abrupt diversion of Rolf's attention. No doubt, to her it was normal dinner conversation, everybody friendly and on a first-name basis.

"That depends, Rolf. Thieves, embezzlers, forgers, I just feel relieved. Here's another man put out of the way before he gets dangerous, one more man stopped short of murder."

"Murder? You think all crime leads to murder?"

Burt put his knife on his plate and weighed his words carefully. "Put it this way, Rolf. Murder is insanity. Crime of any kind is a small dose of the same thing."

"Oh, I don't agree. The profit motive—"

"—is an excuse they give themselves. Show me a financially successful crook, and I'll show you a man who could have made just as much money in, say, the used-car business. Why did he turn to crime? Social protest. The hell with everybody, he says, I won't play their stinking game. So he commits a crime and gets away with it. Why don't they catch me? he wonders. He commits another, then another, getting bolder and bolder until he's finally caught and tossed in the pen. Then he's relieved as hell. See, he says to himself, I was right. Everybody's out to get me."

Rolf was smiling. "And if he isn't caught, I suppose he finally commits murder."

Burt shrugged. "That's the biggest social protest of all."

"Yes." Rolf pursed his lips thoughtfully. "Interesting to meet a philosophical cop. How do you feel when you get a murderer?"

"I feel good, Rolf. Damn good. I feel I'm saving a life, maybe several. Because they don't generally stop at one. It's like getting an olive out of a bottle, the first one's the hardest. After that it becomes a simple and final solution to everything. Even the simplest irritation, a waitress spills a drink on your lap and your first thought is, kill her."

"Burt," said Joss. "That's insane."

"That's my point. A sane man might, under very pressing circumstances, commit one murder. But he wouldn't stay sane long. Murder's too big a load to carry. Even your Nazi friends, Rolf, had to keep telling themselves they were just following orders."

"And when a cop kills?" asked Rolf softly.

Burt felt the hair rise on the back of his neck. "What do you mean?"

"I mean, what kind of fiction does a cop provide himself with when he kills—"

Joss cut in quickly. "Rolf, I want to show you something."

Rolf ignored her. He leaned forward and fixed his eyes on Burt. "*I* know what they tell themselves. They say it was an unavoidable accident. I aimed for his legs but somebody jostled my gun. I fired over his head but he jumped up and caught the bullet. He was trying to kill me and I had to stop him." He leaned back, looking pleased with himself. "I have a theory about cops, Burt. They know, when they go into the racket, that eventually they're going to find themselves in a position to kill legally—"

Joss rose. "Rolf, come over here a minute."

"Let me finish," said Rolf with sudden peevishness. "You see what I'm getting at, Burt?"

Burt felt sticky perspiration beneath his clothes. At the beginning of Rolf's soliloquy he had thought, Well, so Rolf's hobby is cop-baiting. He'd been over this route before and, rather than anger, had felt only a faint boredom. But now the man was dealing with the subconscious motives of a policeman who kills, and these were the precise questions Burt had been asking himself.

"Rolf, joining the police doesn't get you a license for killing—"

"How many cops have burned for it?"

"Rolf, I want to talk to you," said Joss.

Rolf sighed and stood up. "My theory is that cops are instinctive killers who've found a socially accepted way of going about it. Think it over."

Burt watched Rolf and Joss walk over to the edge and pretend to be looking through the telescope. Joss would no doubt tell him about the boy, and Burt would have preferred that she mind her own business. But of course Joss would say it was her business to see that no misunderstandings arose between guests.

Well, unfinished business, Mrs. Rolf Keener. "Could I borrow your comb?" he asked.

She looked up in surprise. "Sure."

She delved into her little handbag and came up with a sequinned comb. She wiped it with a napkin and gave it to him. He saw with dismay that it was clean of hair. Scratch one effort. . . .

He combed his hair and gave it back. "The temperature has cooled since last night," he said casually.

And just as casually she replied, "I threw you the ball and you dropped it. You want to pick it up again?"

He had only to stir the ashes.

"I just wanted to say, if you need help with anything, tell me before he gets back."

He'd been thinking about the letters, but she pointed a finger at the untouched pigeon on his plate. "You can. Slip that under the table to me, quick."

There are times when a man gets involved in a scene so bizarre that he must freeze his intellect, numb his mental process, before he can act. It was in this way that Burt passed her the pigeon and sat listening to the hidden crackle of tiny bones and the juicy sound of her mastication. She ate with her head lowered, devouring the entire pigeon in the time it took to rip off the meat and convey it to her mouth. Burt sat with a growing conviction that he was the only sane person at the table. Finished, she touched a napkin to her mouth with such incongruous delicacy that he burst out laughing.

She frowned toward Rolf, then leaned confidentially across the table. "Don't tell Rolf. He's trying to enforce my diet."

A bright light flashed in his brain. "Oh, you've put on weight recently?"

"You think I'm getting fat?"

"I see nothing wrong with your shape, if your clothes only fit—"

"Oh, that's *part* of it, don't you see? He's got this idea that people go through life trying to balance out their various urges. I've got an urge to eat, but I've also got this urge to wear nice things. He decided that the urge to dress well was strongest. So he went out and bought me a raft of lovely clothes for our trip, only they're two sizes too small. He figures I'll diet in order to be able to wear them; meanwhile I'm on the edge of a nervous breakdown because I'm afraid something's going to burst out any minute."

Burt managed a faint smile. The whole ridiculous story fitted Rolf's weird logic. Unfortunately, one of the main props in his theory was that the clothes weren't really hers. . . .

Joss and Rolf returned, and Joss said she'd see if the boys were ready to play music. Burt excused himself and followed her out to the kitchen.

"Joss, I wonder if you'd take your eyes off Rolf long enough to listen to Mrs. Keener. I want to know if her voice sounds . . . different than when she first came."

She looked at Burt with unfocused eyes. "I couldn't tell from the grunts she's given so far."

Burt frowned. "Yeah, that's funny. After you left she talked up a storm."

"Don't forget her husband left, too."

"What does that mean?"

"Oh, come now. Does a woman camp out where her old man can see? No, baby. She sits quiet and sedate and something like a stick until he gets out of earshot. Then she turns it on." Joss smiled loosely and patted his cheek. "That chick's got her net out for you, Burtie. Don't get tangled up in it."

Burt realized that Joss was half-drunk and a bad security risk, but he needed help.

"Listen, when we go back out there, I want you to get everybody to sign the guestbook. I'm particularly interested in Mrs. Keener."

She raised her brows. "What's on your mind?"

"Just a sneaky way to see her handwriting." He patted her shoulder. "Go on, play it natural. I'll explain when the party's over."

Back at the table, Joss carried it off ... almost. She brought up the subject of a previous guest, forgot his name, then got the guest book, a massive bookkeeping ledger, to refresh her memory. She discovered that none of those present had signed the book. Burt signed first, then Rolf Keener, who asked Joss with a faint smile, "Is it okay if I sign for both of us?"

Joss shot Burt a brief glance, then said quickly, "Oh, no. Everybody sign."

Rolf, still smiling, pushed the heavy book in front of the woman. "Here, Mrs. Rolf Keener. Sergeant March would like your autograph."

Burt met the cold blue eyes and regretted his maneuver with the book. He'd revealed more than he could ever learn, and it gave him no surprise to look across the table and see the woman print in block capitals: MRS. ROLF KEENER.

The boys began playing a bouncy local mixture of calypso, cha-cha-cha, and Latin American rock-and-roll. They'd donned white shirts for the occasion, and Boris managed to look dignified even with a nose-flute in one flaring nostril. Coco sat on the floor with his legs hooked around a pair of bongo drums. His hands, pink-scarred by fish-bites, fluttered like black wings on the taut drum-skin. Godfrey's face hung vacuous over a guitar almost as large as himself.

Rolf pulled Joss up to dance on the wooden floor; he acted like someone playing a hilarious game—and winning it. Burt hesitated to trust his leg, but when Joss and Rolf began their third twist, he asked Mrs. Keener to dance.

"If I pop out of my dress," she said, getting up, "will you look the other way?"

"We'll have to wait and see," said Burt.

Burt found to his surprise that he enjoyed dancing with her. She moved with a boneless, sinuous grace which never brought her into contact with him, but nevertheless made him totally aware of her body. He glanced down at her muscular calves, saw that her feet were shod in flat-heeled, ballet-style slippers.

"Did you used to be a professional dancer?"

She dimpled in a way she must have practiced. "You say the nicest things."

Burt thought: She's certainly no junkie. She's a healthy female animal with beautiful coordination, a gargantuan appetite, and none of the addict's sexual apathy. He could feel her physical warmth surrounding him like a blanket. On their third dance he spoke softly in her ear: "On the slope behind your cabin, there's a concrete water catchment with a tile-roofed cistern at the lower end. Have you seen it?"

"Yes." She whirled away once and came back into his arms. "In an hour?"

So simple, he thought, like meeting her for coffee. "That's fine."

She came against him for an instant as though sealing the bargain with a sample. Burt found himself looking over her head into the icy blue eyes of Rolf. There was no jealousy there, only a crinkle of mild amusement.

But then, he asked himself, why should Rolf be jealous? For he had just learned, with a certainty that dispelled all doubt, that the woman in his arms was not Tracy Keener.

The woman pleaded a headache fifteen minutes later and the pair left despite Joss's protest that parties didn't end this way in the islands. Joss decided to stay and finish the wine and Burt stayed with her.

"Joss, what's the best way to get to this island without the authorities knowing?"

"In the hold of a ship, I guess."

Burt thought of Mrs. Keener's tight clothing, he'd returned to the theory that they'd belonged to a smaller woman. She couldn't have carried much luggage as a stowaway.

"Is there a quicker way?"

"Flying in at Grenada."

"She'd go through immigration."

"Not our immigration. We come under St. Vincent, the southern islands come under Grenada. People cross all the time and nobody knows unless they get in trouble."

"Then Rolf could have picked her up in the launch from Grenada. Of course."

"Who, Mrs. Keener?"

"She isn't Mrs. Keener."

Joss's mouth dropped open. "You mean he sent his girl friend down here—"

"I mean that the woman who came on O'Ryan's schooner is not the woman we had dinner with tonight. There's been a switch, and it happened sometime between last night and the night before."

She stared at him a moment, then shook her head. "I've had too much to drink, Burt. I can't figure it."

"Okay. I searched the purse while I was on the schooner. Her driver's license said she was five-feet-four, and weighed a hundred and five pounds. Now this woman was nearer one-twenty, wouldn't you say?"

"At least, but women change their weight."

"But not their height, Joss. While we were dancing I noticed that she was wearing low heels. The top of her head came to the tip of my nose. I'm six feet and a quarter inch tall. My nose is approximately five inches below the top of my head. That would put her height at about five-seven."

"But why? To change wives—"

"Divorce is a lot less trouble. It's bigger than that, and I've got a feeling there's a lot of money involved, knowing Rolf."

"What are you going to do?"

"Get more information—maybe. I've got a date with her out by the cistern."

Joss looked alarmed. "Burt, it's probably a trap."

"I know. I don't aim to throw myself at her feet without looking around. Rolf has a gun, you know."

"Burt, don't risk it. Look, let me talk to Rolf, I'll tell him I'm sick, get him to take me to St. Vincent, go to the police—"

"And tell them what?"

"Why . . . that there's a woman here—"

"And our proof?"

"My word—"

"Have you told anybody about seeing your husband on the beach wearing hip boots?"

"What does that—?" She closed her mouth, reddening. "Oh, I see what you mean. They'd think I was raving. Okay, you go."

"Suppose Rolf does have a big deal on; he'd see that I never got to St. Vincent."

Joss laughed nervously. "Oh, hell, this thing has sobered me up quicker than a gallon of black coffee. Who do you suppose the woman is?"

"It's not important, is it? I'm wondering what happened to the real Mrs. Keener."

FIVE

Burt squatted inside a clump of grass and peered at the woman who stood beside the cistern. Strange that she'd wear her white beach coat to a secret tryst; she stood out like neon beneath the thick crescent of the moon. The water catchment was a gray triangle on the slope above her. He could hear rats chittering in the grass around him; the booming surf had become an unchanging part of life, audible only when he made an effort to hear it. Beyond the cistern he saw the fumaroles geysering up like pale gleaming wraiths in the moonlight.

A match flared and went out. A cigarette glowed in the pale oval of her face, brightened and dimmed several times in rapid succession. Lover's getting impatient, he thought, but I'll bet she doesn't leave. . . .

A cloud obscured the moon and darkened the island. A darker shadow joined the white shape of the woman. When the moon came out again, the larger shadow broke away and disappeared around the corner of the cistern. Burt gripped the two-foot length of steel pipe and crept out of the grass. He angled to the right, down the slope and back up again on the side of the cistern opposite the woman. He peered around the corner and saw Rolf squatting with his back to the stone wall. Rolf was an old night fighter; Burt knew he could never sneak close enough for a solid blow. He picked up a stone and, holding his arm away from his body so there would be no swish of cloth, threw it over Rolf's head. It thumped on the ground ten feet ahead of the man; Rolf rose to his feet. Burt leaped forward and swung the pipe against his head with a delicate, calculated force. Rolf fell against the cistern and started a limp-

© Lorillard 1975

Come for the filter...

A PRODUCT OF
Lorillard

KENT
WITH
THE FAMOUS MICRONITE FILTER

DELUXE LENGTH

legged slide to the ground; Burt caught him beneath the arms and lowered him gently. He withdrew a .38 snub-nosed revolver from Rolf's shoulder holster and shoved it in his hip pocket. Rolf's pulse and breathing were both surprisingly normal; Burt decided he'd have less than a quarter hour with the woman.

He retraced his steps around the cistern to where she waited. Like a passenger whose bus has just arrived, she pushed herself away from the wall and threw her cigarette to the ground. As she came toward him, Burt saw that her long legs were bare beneath the beach coat.

"I was beginning to get cold," she said, locking her hands behind his head and looking up with a teasing smile. "I wondered if you'd have the guts to come."

Burt spread his hands across her back and felt the muscle-taut flesh beneath it. She was not as calm as she appeared.

"Where'd you leave Rolf?" he asked.

"In the cabin, reading. He thinks I'm taking a walk." She rocked against him, an undulating warmth pressing him from chest to knee. "We don't have much time. Will you kiss me?"

"No biting?"

"Maybe that comes later."

He felt the surprising coolness of her lips and the curiously facile, impersonal probing of her tongue. He tasted wine and braised pigeon, and decided that this girl knew all the right moves at the right time, but that skill could never take the place of natural passion.

Then suddenly all her weight hung from his neck. She fell backward onto the ground, pulling him off-balance so that he had to put out both hands to avoid crushing her with his weight. The sandy soil scraped his elbows as he tried to break her grip around his neck, and Burt discovered that somewhere in midfall she had managed to unfasten the robe. He made three more discoveries in rapid succession: She wore nothing beneath the robe, she had a wiry masculine strength, and whatever her ulterior purpose in arranging the meeting, the seduction was in deadly earnest.

He jerked free and sat back on his haunches. "Cool it a minute. What's all the rush?"

She put her hands behind her head and began laughing softly.

"Did him want to chat? Did him want to be a big strong man and just overwhelm poor little me?"

Her mock babytalk curdled his stomach. "I think I get it. Rolf was supposed to catch me in the act and shoot me, right?"

She raised her head and frowned at him. "Huh?"

Burt rose to his feet. "Get up. I'll show you something."

"Oh, now wait—"

Burt seized her arm and jerked her up. "Come on."

Rolf was stirring when they rounded the corner. The woman tore free and ran toward him. "Rolf, what happened?" She knelt beside him an instant, then whirled and leaped at Burt, her teeth bared, her white robe flying out like the wings of a silver moth on both sides of her nude body. Her nails raked his cheek once, then again, while Burt wrestled with an untimely question: Where does a gentleman seize a naked woman he doesn't want to hurt? He felt he was being smothered in satin-firm flesh, she seemed to have a dozen arms, breasts, stomachs all heavy with an exciting smell of sweat and perfume. Her teeth were seeking a purchase somewhere in the region of his jugular vein when he found her shoulders and pushed with all his strength. She sprawled backward on the ground, but she was game; she bounced up and was about to charge again when Rolf's voice cracked like a pistol shot:

"Drop it, Bunny!"

She stopped as though on a short leash, her robe hanging open. Rolf sat up, drew his legs under him, and spoke in a tired voice:

"Wrap up the package, baby. It didn't sell."

She drew her robe together and tied it slowly, like a child putting away a doll which she'd been forbidden to play with until Christmas. Burt watched the pair, feeling like a stranger at a family dinner.

"It wasn't my fault," she said with petulance.

"Mine. Totally mine." Rolf touched the back of his head. "Sergeant March used an old trick. I was expecting something more original." He pressed his hand to the bulge of his jacket, sighed, and looked up at Burt. "Did you borrow my gun, old man?"

"I'll keep it for a while."

Rolf smiled. "With my compliments. I don't like guns. That one shoots slightly to the left, anyway." He fumbled beneath his jacket and drew out a cigarette. "Will you ask your question here, Sergeant, or—" he paused to ignite the cigarette "—shall we go to my cabin and have a drink?"

"This is fine." Burt pulled out the gun and squatted with his back against the wall. To the woman he said, "Get over beside him."

She obeyed, leaning against Rolf and delving into his jacket for a cigarette. She lit it from Rolf's and giggled softly. "Maybe he handles a gun better than he does a woman."

"Keep quiet," said Rolf absently. "Permit me to observe, March, that any restriction of an individual's freedom of movement is technically kidnapping. Since you're off-duty and outside the United States, you have no authority whatever."

"Let's all go together and complain to the authorities."

Rolf chuckled. "You win. First question."

"Where's your wife?"

"Sitting beside me."

"You called her Bunny."

"A term of endearment, just between us."

Burt decided it felt good to have the intellectual jump on Rolf. He smiled. "The island seems to have agreed with her. She's grown three-and-a-half inches since she arrived."

Rolf stiffened and looked sharply at the woman.

"Rolf, I didn't—"

"No, I understand it now." He turned back to Burt. "I assumed you'd be too chivalrous to search the purse. I was wrong." He pressed a shaky hand to the back of his neck. "Do me, Bunny. I've got a headache." She rose to her knees behind him and began kneading his neck. Rolf looked at Burt. "She's Bunny DeVore, specialty dancer, late of Miami Beach. She starts her dance in a cowboy suit and winds up wearing only a gun. Clever act, particularly when she demonstrates the symbolism of the gun—"

"You didn't bring her here to dance," said Burt.

"No, she goes with me on all my trips to South America. Sort of a traveling secretary, except that she can't type and can't take shorthand." He chuckled. "Pity you struck so soon, March; you'd have learned what makes her so valuable in my business."

"I know," said Burt, "But I can't say I dig the professional touch."

"Oh, you lousy fink—"

"Go to the cabin, Bunny," said Rolf. Your ego's getting noisy."

"Stay there," said Burt.

"Burt's afraid you'd bring back a sawed-off shotgun, I suppose." To Burt he said: "I'm your hostage, so why worry? I can speak more freely when she's gone."

Burt hesitated a moment, then nodded. Bunny rose and disappeared into the darkness, her back stiff.

"She minds well," observed Burt.

The secret," said Rolf, "is to give no commands she's not already half-inclined to follow. She usually enjoys the tasks I give her. This one tonight—I must say she was particularly eager, but now—you know what they say about a woman spurned. I'd watch my back if I were you."

"What was the purpose of this business tonight?"

"I have a theory that people act because of pressure on them. When I want somebody to do something, I find out what pressures prevent them from doing it. Then I set up a counterpressure in my favor, stronger than the one against."

"And Bunny supplied the pressure."

"There are less pleasant pressures, March."

Burt narrowed his eyes; Rolf didn't seem to be threatening, only stating a fact. "I had a feeling last night you wanted something from me. Why not just tell me what it is?"

"Not until you put the gun away."

"All right. Then it can wait. Tell me why you pulled the switch."

"That was a challenging problem. My wife and Bunny are almost polar opposites. My wife is small, as you know, with a triangular face, brown eyes, blue-black hair and a faintly olive complexion. Bunny is a type particularly favored by South Americans, an ash blonde with green eyes—"

"*Green?* But they were brown—"

"Tinted contact lenses."

"Oh . . . is that why her eyes watered?"

"They do when she first puts them in. Later the tears stop." He ground out his cigarette in the dirt. "Of course it was easy to dye her hair, but that left the problems of weight and complexion. I put Bunny on a strict diet and told her to get tanned in a hurry. Meanwhile she wore dark glasses and stayed out of sight. Joss couldn't see well. I remembered that, and I figured that white women look basically alike to the native boys. The fact that my wife seldom makes close friends made the problem simpler. I told Bunny not to talk to Joss at the start, for fear the woman would recognize the change in her voice. Gradually Bunny would show more and more of herself, until the reality of her presence replaced the memory of my wife." Rolf sighed. "The only thing we couldn't change was Bunny's height. Now that's all I'll tell you until you put the gun away."

Burt held onto the gun; he didn't feel he needed it any more, but he couldn't put it aside without losing part of the initiative.

"I can tell you a few things," said Burt. "You pulled the switch night before last, didn't you?"

Rolf shrugged. "Think what you like."

"She flew in to Grenada and you picked her up in the launch, brought her here, and removed your wife. What did you do, kill her?"

Rolf looked up, startled. "Of course not."

"Then let me see her."

"No."

Burt paused. "Did Bunny come in as Tracy Keener?"

Rolf hesitated, then nodded. "You'd have a hard time proving which one was real. Bunny's papers are foolproof."

"Still the authorities would be interested to learn that two Tracy Keeners were on the island at the same time."

"It would be embarrassing," admitted Rolf, "should Grenada and St. Vincent ever compare notes, but hardly enough to excuse your taking me in at gunpoint. I can promise you this, Burt: should you try it, I could produce my wife within a few hours, and she would be in good health. She would swear that she left this island of her own free will, and has remained away only because she wanted to. And there you would stand with egg on your face."

Burt believed him; Rolf could produce his wife within a few hours. That meant . . . well, hell, it meant she could be anywhere, on the big islands of St. Vincent or Grenada, or on any one of a hundred smaller clods of land. It would take a month to search everywhere, even if he had a boat. And he didn't have a boat.

"If your wife is not a prisoner," said Burt, "what's to keep her from deciding to take off?"

"Pressure," said Rolf.

"What kind of pressure?"

"The most irresistible kind," said Rolf with a faint smile. "It comes from inside her."

Burt felt a chill climb his back; it seemed inconceivable that a man would turn his wife into a heroin addict merely in order to control her. But then, with Rolf, nothing was impossible.

Burt shoved the gun back in his hip pocket. "I suppose your wife knows Bunny took her place."

"She knows it's for her own good."

"How's that?"

"To remove her from danger."

"Danger on this island?"

Rolf nodded.

Burt frowned. "You could have left her at home."

"They'd know where to find her."

"Who's they?"

"I am . . . involved in a deal which puts me in considerable danger. My wife could be a means of getting to me."

"Yes, but if the masquerade works, doesn't that put Bunny in the same danger?"

"She's less sensitive to danger than my wife. And she knows how high the stakes are."

"How high?"

"Mmmm. Say the liquid assets of a certain small Latin American government in exile." Rolf leaned forward. "Interested?"

"What do I have to do?"

"Be my bodyguard while I'm here on the island."

Burt smiled. "You don't need a bodyguard."

"You're wrong. I'm an offensive fighter. I haven't the patience to guard my back. Besides, if they come, there'll be more than one."

"And I'm to capture them and take them to jail?"

Rolf laughed aloud. "Extradition papers, that sort of thing? Don't be silly."

"Then you expect me to kill them."

"You'd find that more practical."

Burt felt his throat tighten. "I'm not a hired gun, Rolf. I'm not even an instinctive killer, despite what Joss may have told you. I'm a cop, and I serve the law. I've been told that's far above any individual interest—"

"No sermons, Burt." Rolf rose to his feet and rubbed

his forehead. "I'm going to get more of Bunny's treatment. We'll talk some more, of course. You haven't heard all of my terms. Maybe you'll find that you have no choice but to defend me."

"More pressure, Rolf? Bunny won't be so eager this time."

"Ah, Burt. There are outside pressures ... and inside pressures. I prefer the latter."

"What does that mean?"

"You're a cop. You've got the gun. Figure it out."

He walked away laughing to himself. A minute later the screen door slammed on cabin two. Burt walked back to the beach club and found it dark and silent except for the squeak and thump of rats fighting over discarded tidbits of food. He stood on the beach and watched Rolf's launch rock in the gentle swell of the lagoon. It would be easy to rewire the ignition and go to St. Vincent and ... what? He still wouldn't know where Tracy Keener was. No doubt she was the reason for Rolf's cruise earlier today; he'd know enough to dole out no more than a day's supply of the drug at a time. The secret of enslaving an addict was to restrict the supply.

So he'd be going again tomorrow.

Burt climbed up to the watchtower and sat on the parapet. He could hear the wind rippling the grass below with a sound like sliding silk. He rubbed his aching leg and thought of Bunny's cool fingers. He tasted her lipstick on his mouth and wondered if it had been all work and no play for her. . . .

A rock clattered. He peered over the parapet into a pair of wide, white eyes. A familiar T-shirt bulged below them.

"Maudie," he whispered. "Go back home."

"*Maman* sleeping. She know nothing."

"Go back anyway."

"Yes, sir."

Burt sat back down inside the tower and leaned against the low wall. A minute later he heard a sound like marbles rattling. He peered over the edge and saw

Maudie huddled against the base of the tower with her arms hugging her stomach.

"Oh, hell. Come on up."

She crawled over the edge and sat down, stretching her warm young body beside him. "I help you watch, sir."

"Uh-huh," said Burt.

Five minutes later the tight-curled mat of her hair fell onto his shoulder. She snored softly. Burt stretched her out on the stones and pillowed her head with his jacket. He felt a wave of warm protectiveness toward the sleeping girl.

Yeah, he thought, that's what Rolf meant. I'm a cop, and I'm hung up with these people. Whether they like it or not, whether they accept it or not, I'm responsible for the safety of everyone on the island: Joss, Maudie, the boys, Jata, Tracy Keener . . . even Rolf and Bunny. Because if the danger which threatens Rolf should threaten the others, I will have to act.

SIX

Dawn came up unpleasantly, with a bleak drizzle which soaked Burt to the skin and rendered Maudie's T-shirt as transparent as onionskin. He sent the girl home and climbed down the hill through dripping grass. Coco sat on the steps of the beach club looking morosely at the rain dripping off the thatched roof.

"Nobody up yet?" asked Burt.

"No, sir." Coco rested his chin in his hands and gazed at Rolf's launch rocking in the rain-peppered lagoon. "My mind tells me he take me fishing today."

"Your mind gives you a bum steer," said Burt. "But I'll give you five bucks to go up to the *piton* and watch where he goes."

"Yes, *sir!*"

The pink soles of Coco's bare feet sent up spurts of wet sand as he ran down the beach. Burt went to his cabin and took a shower, then put on dry clothes and lay down on his bed fully dressed. The damp weather had brought throbbing pain to his leg; he seemed to be able to sleep only a half-hour when a spurt of pain would awaken him, and he would lie with cold sweat soaking his clothes while he tried to arrange his leg in a more comfortable position. He was doing this for the fifth or the tenth time when a shot blasted just outside his cabin. Burt was off his bed and on the floor when the second report came. He ran out onto the porch with Rolf's .38 in his hand and looked up to see a graceful frigate bird falter in flight, then begin a slow downward glide which ended in a splash far out to sea.

Burt lowered his eyes and saw the two men on the narrow beach just below his cabin. One carried a gun over his shoulder, holding it by the barrel in defiance of all gun safety rules. The other had broken open a double-barreled shotgun and was feeding in new shells. Burt shoved the .38 in his hip pocket and strode down to the beach. He'd forgotten the twinge in his leg; his ears burned with unreasoning rage.

"Hey!" he shouted.

The man who held the gun by the barrel turned to frown at Burt. He was a stocky, dark man who looked immensely powerful, with heavy, black-furred arms and a pelt of black hair poking through the neck of his crackling new sport shirt. The other man, also dressed in new sport shirt and trousers, was bigger but more loosely built. He raised his shotgun and scanned the sky, ignoring Burt.

"Why the hell did you shoot a frigate bird?" asked Burt.

The hairy man flashed a broad unconvincing smile and held out his hand. "I'm Ace Smith. Real-estate operator. This is one of my associates, Hoke Farnum."

Burt didn't take his hand. He'd always had a low opinion of men who killed for pleasure. These two didn't even seem to be having fun. "I asked you why you shot the frigate bird."

Ace Smith shrugged and waved at the other man. "Hoke thought it was a pigeon. We came here to shoot pigeons."

Burt glanced at Hoke. He had a thick fleshy head topped with coarse black hair. His face appeared the color and texture of pie dough with the features pressed in place by blunt fingers. The man didn't smile; he didn't look as though he knew how. He looked at Burt from eyes that could have been dried prunes floating in skimmed milk for all the emotion they showed, then turned away and drew a bead on a pelican bobbing in the swell just beyond the surf line. Burt leaped forward and knocked down the gun barrel. "Fool! Don't you know a pelican when you see one?"

The big man backed away with surprised annoyance. He gave Burt a puzzled look, then turned to Ace. "Who is this guy, the local game warden?"

"Bird lover," said the other. "Shoot what you want. They don't enforce game laws here."

For an instant the scene froze, with Burt facing the two armed men. Hoke's gun was a twelve-gauge shotgun; Ace carried an over-under model, twenty-gauge shotgun below, thirty-caliber rifle above.

Burt felt his skin draw tight; he hadn't smelled gunpowder since that night in the jewelry store.

He forced himself to relax; no use getting somebody killed over a frigate bird.

"You're the Smith who reserved two cabins?" he asked.

"Uh-yeah." Ace's smile was gone; like a rubber mask the face had snapped back into a taut, watchful pattern. There was violence in his eyes, but it was different from Rolf's, nearer to the surface, more defensive and, probably, with a quicker boiling point.

"How'd you two great white hunters get on the island?"

"Charter boat," said Ace.

As Burt turned to scan the shoreline, Ace said, "He left hours ago."

Burt looked up and saw the pale disc of the sun shining through the haze directly overhead. It was past noon. . . .

He left the two men and walked to the club. The cruiser was gone, as he'd expected. Godfrey, who was raking debris off the beach in front of the club, said the man and the woman had left right after breakfast. Boris was polishing the bar with an oiled cloth. To the left of the club, Joss lay in a hammock strung between two palm trees cuddling a rum punch on her stomach. Her eyes were closed, her mouth slightly open.

The tranquil scene gave Burt a queasy feeling, as though they were all sitting on the edge of a volcano, and he was the only one who could hear the rumble of the approaching eruption.

He walked up to her hammock and rocked it gently. She jumped, and liquid sloshed out of her glass and dampened the mound of her stomach.

"Burt, what—?"

"Why'd you let those new men in?"

"Boris put them up," she said, taking a sip from her glass. "I was asleep when they came in from Grenada."

"Asleep or passed out?"

"Well . . . rum makes me sleepy."

"Sure, when you drink a quart of it." He reached out and took the glass from her hand.

"Now Burt, listen—"

"You listen, Joss. I need help. I can't depend on you when you're juiced out of your mind." He set the glass on the sand beside her hammock. "Now, how many gorillas are there?"

She looked wistfully at the glass, then sighed. "Well, there were supposed to be four, but Boris said there were only three. That Mr. Smith is in cabin three, the other two are in cabin four—" She stopped abruptly. "What do you mean, gorillas?"

"I mean gorillas, gunmen, torpedoes, hoods. I've seen enough of them in lineups to know the type."

She turned pale. "But why . . . on this island—?"

"Tell me, did their reservations come in before or after Rolf's?"

"Neither. O'Ryan drops the mail off once a week. Both letters were in the same batch."

"So many visitors during hurricane season could hardly be an accident. Two and two adds up to four. Four against one."

"Four? You're not including Rolf?"

"Why not? They came in from Grenada, the same as the phony Mrs. Keener."

"Ah, that one." Joss's eyes narrowed. "She kept her date last night?"

Burt nodded.

"And you . . . did you enjoy yourself?"

Burt touched a finger to the faint scratches on his cheek. "I could have, if I'd wanted to perform for an audience." Briefly he related what had happened, including Rolf's hints of danger and a vast fortune at stake. Joss's reaction was surprising, but typical. She swung her legs to the ground and spoke with prim indignation:

"I'm going to the police and have the woman thrown out. That kind of promiscuity is just not allowed on my island."

Burt shook his head slowly. "We've been over this ground before, Joss. How would you go?"

"Rolf—"

"You'd never get there."

"Burt, don't be silly. Rolf wouldn't ... I mean, he could be involved in a shady deal, like you say, but he wouldn't hurt a woman."

Burt smiled. "I envy you, Joss. Your feminine intuition would be such a help in detective work."

"Oh, it's more definite than that. We talked about the stars last night. He's a Leo, a perfect Leo. He's not bound by a lot of stifling rules, he's a leader . . ."

Burt stared as she talked, amazed that the accident of a man's birthday could outweigh all contrary evidence. True, it helped that Rolf was handsome, likable and intelligent, and that Joss was slightly sex-starved.

He decided not to argue with her. It wouldn't hurt to let her think Rolf was harmless, as long as the man didn't start using her for his own purposes. In any case, Burt wasn't eager to shatter Rolf's good-guy pose; he had a feeling that could only unleash a chain reaction of violence.

"Okay," he said finally. "I could be wrong about Rolf. But not about these other guys. Stay clear of them."

"I'll do better than that. I'll ask them to leave."

Burt sighed. "Here we are again. How will they go? Their launch left."

"Why, Rolf will take them off when he gets back."

Burt smiled slowly. "Go ahead and ask him. I'll be curious to see how he gets out of it."

Burt found Boris in the kitchen scratching his wispy goatee and grumbling about the food supply. The mountain of stores which Joss had hinted at consisted of three cases of Argentine canned beef and twenty-four tins of ship's biscuits. That would have been fine, Boris explained, if they'd had their usual fare of birds and seafood, but there could be no fishing without a boat, the surf was too high to get lobsters and sea snails from the reef, and the gunshots had driven all the pigeons to the highest crags.

"Maybe tonight I hold a manicou," said Boris. "But for now . . ."

Burt sat down to a breakfast of bully beef and biscuits. The biscuits rattled against his teeth, as hard and tasteless as C-ration crackers. The beef was stringy, blood-red, and so salty he used a quart of water to wash it down. He pushed back his plate and saw Boris watching him with an expression of deep sympathy.

"You were here when those new men came in?" Burt asked.

Boris shook his head. "I was up on the hill making charcoal, when I hear the boat. I do not move, for I think the blond man returning early. When I come down, the men are in their cabins. They do not let me in to open windows, show them how the bath works. I think they do not wish to give me a tip?"

The last sentence ended on a rising, querulous inflection. Burt didn't think the men were concerned about tipping; a passion for secrecy was exactly what he'd have expected after seeing the pair on the beach. It was sheer luck that they'd got on to the island without being seen. The puzzle was that only three men had arrived to occupy reservations made for four. What had happened to the fourth man?

"Godfrey didn't see them?" asked Burt.

"No, sir. I send him up to the rocks to look for bird's eggs."

"How about Coco—? Oh, hell!"

He jumped to his feet and left the club. The new arrivals had driven Coco completely from his mind.

Burt found Coco lying on his back with his white hat shading his face. Burt jerked it off:

"Did you see a launch leave three men on the island?"

Coco blinked and sat up, wiping his mouth with the back of his hand. "No, sir."

Burt threw the hat back with disgust. "That nap just cost you five bucks, Coco."

"But, sir! I watch where the other go, as you told me." He scrambled to his knees and pointed to the south. "I follow them with my eyes until they pass out of sight around that island, called Ram Island."

"Could they have stopped there?"

"No anchorage on that side. Only on this side."

"What's behind it?"

"Oh, many, many islands . . ." He named a dozen before Burt stopped him.

"The Tobago Cays. Isn't that a group of very small islands off to themselves?"

"Yes, sir. Petit Rameau, Petit Bateau, Jamesby, Baradal and Petit Tabac." Coco was obviously enjoying the chance to display his knowledge.

"Anybody live there?"

"No, sir. Sometimes boats come from Barbados, people stay there on holiday, swim, fish. Sometimes fishermen stop to dry fish for market, eat turtle. But they must bring food and water—"

"They don't visit during this season, do they?"

"No, sir. When the sea high, current rush through very swif'. Many rocks."

Burt thought about it: If Rolf wanted to keep his wife out of sight, he'd have to find a place where nobody would be likely to stumble onto her. She wouldn't know enough to stay out of sight when she was all hyped-up on junk, and that way he'd be damn sure she couldn't take off and try to score on her own—

Coco's shout interrupted his thoughts. He looked down to see the cruiser coming from the east. Now what the hell? Burt wondered. *That clever devil has circled around and come back a different way, and now I'm not sure of anything.* He felt frustration pinch his nostrils as he watched the cruiser approach, trailing a long wake and cleaving the water with two high bow waves. She was a powerful craft; she could probably outrun anything but a U.S. coast-guard cutter.

He watched Rolf ease up to the edge of the lagoon. The entrance was tricker than ever, but conversely less dangerous. The swells were higher, but if you were a good enough boatman to catch the top of a swell, your chances of getting snagged were that much smaller. Burt found himself holding his breath as the launch disappeared in white water; then letting it out as the boat reappeared gleaming wet, in the lagoon. He had to admire Rolf's dexterity with the wheel, and he wondered where he'd learned it.

Burt stayed on the tower and watched Joss meet Rolf at the jetty. While the two talked, Bunny disappeared in the direction of the cabins, walking as though she were very, very tired. The two pigeon hunters had paused in front of the beach club to watch the landing, now, perhaps in response to Rolf's call, they joined Rolf and Joss at the jetty. Burt climbed down from the tower and descended the hill. He reached the beach just as Joss slapped her hands against her hips and left the beach. Rolf gave Burt a mock, half-smiling salute as he approached.

"New fellows for the club, Burt. I offered them a lift to Bequia but they're afraid of the sea."

Ace hunched his shoulders and glared at Burt. "Like I told her, I'll leave. But after that last trip out here, I ain't ready to go again so soon."

"I've gone through rougher water than this," said Rolf, looking like a dashing cinema adventurer with his hair wet and drops of water clinging to his mustache. "In the Strait of Gibraltar, with gunboats chasing me."

"Well, I didn't. When the sea calms down I'll take your offer, if she's still got her mind made up . . ."

And Burt had a strange feeling that both men were playing parts for his benefit . . .

. . . When, from the nearest cabin, came what sounded like a ragged moan. Burt started forward, but Ace was standing in front of him with the gun in the crook of his arm. "Hold it, that's only Charlie. He has nightmares." His smile returned, too broad to be real, and he spoke over his shoulder. "Hoke, go turn Charlie over on his stomach."

Burt felt rage boiling inside him, but forced himself to speak in a quiet voice. "Smith, you act like a damn fool with that gun."

The hairy man raised his brows. "Yeah? You know a lot about guns, bird lover?"

"I know if you don't take it out of my stomach, I'll feed it to you."

Ace eyed Burt curiously. "What did you say your name was?"

"Burt March."

"March. Whaddaya do?"

"I sell insurance. And I'll give you five seconds to move that gun. One, two, three—"

"Smith!" Rolf's voice cracked. "You're not the only one who's armed. Do what he says."

Ace looked surprised, then shrugged and smiled at Burt. "Insurance salesman, huh? The island's full of tough nuts." He slung the gun to his shoulder. "I came here to shoot pigeons, and that's what I'll do, as long as people leave me alone."

He turned and walked up the hill, ostentatiously scanning the sky. Burt turned to Rolf. "I'd thank you, but I think you had your own reasons. You had to let him know I had a gun, didn't you?"

"I figured it would save his life. Or yours." Rolf smiled. "Why so disappointed? Did you want to kill him?"

"I wouldn't have killed him. He was standing too close; it wouldn't have been hard to disarm him."

"Yes, and when he came at you with his bare hands? He looks strong as a gorilla."

"I can defend myself."

Rolf shook his head slowly. "I'm glad I didn't decide to be a cop. You've tied your hands, haven't you? You have to let the other man make the first move."

He turned and started away, but Burt called after him. "Rolf, are those the men you think will kill you?"

Rolf paused and waved up at the peak. "Take a look. You think he's hunting pigeons?"

Burt followed his gaze and watched Ace settle himself on the lookout rock with the gun across his knees. He was looking down, his hard face impassive. Burt was reminded of the guard on a prison farm.

SEVEN

The afternoon sizzled by like a slow fuse. Rolf said something about fouled plugs and began dissecting the innards of his cruiser, managing to get romantically grease-stained in the process. Burt had the chilling thought that he was deliberately putting his boat out of action. Joss sat in a wicker armchair at the corner of the club, scanning the sea through her ancient tripod-telescope.

"O'Ryan should be here if he's coming," she told Burt.

"Does he come when it's rough?"

"Never has, but he might."

Bunny came out into the open without her dark glasses, wearing a halter and short-shorts which lacked a couple of inches of doing the job they were meant to do. She paced the beach like a caged tigress for a half-hour, went for a swim in the lagoon, then emerged to lie on her stomach in the sand. She unfastened her halter strap to leave her back bare. Burt could see two inches of milk-white flesh between the top of her shorts and the faint pinkness of her back. There was an engaging dimple on each side of her lower spine.

Burt wasn't the only one who noticed: Ace sat on the steps of the club flicking bits of coral at the sand crabs who scuttled sideways across the sand. He wasn't watching the crabs; he was watching Bunny through lowered bushy brows, like a fullback about to charge the line. Hoke had taken his place on the tower with the gun across his knees.

Joss left her telescope and walked behind the bar; she stood there glaring in Bunny's direction and sneaking quick gulps of rum. Boris stood beside her, pretending not to notice.

Burt tasted the bile of frustration in his throat. What can you do? he wondered. We're prisoners, but does Joss know it, or Boris and the boys? One of them might make a false step and trigger the violence. Well, he thought, you can't hold them all in the palm of your hand. Best you can do is quarantine them.

He went to Joss and persuaded her that she was tired and sleepy, then he walked her up to her house and left her stretched out on the bed with her glass beside her. He took Coco and Godfrey to the south shore of the island and asked if they'd noticed anything odd about the three new arrivals.

"Big men," said Godfrey.

"They don't wish to fish," said Coco.

"They're gunmen," said Burt. "Professional killers. You boys stay clear of them, hear?"

They nodded gravely.

"We may have to leave the island in a hurry. You boys go around and gather up all the dry wood you can find. Carry the little stuff up the hill in case we need a signal fire. The big stuff you can put right here. When the sea goes down, we'll build a raft."

The two deployed up the slope, scanning the ground, and Burt went to find Jata. She lived in a black shingle structure not more than eight feet square, hidden beneath a dark, brooding manchineel tree. He knocked and announced himself. A bolt slid back, a chain rattled, and Jata's glittering eye appeared at a crack in the door. "Sir, I don't come out 'til bad men leave."

"You're on the stick, Jata. Where's Maudie?"

"She sneakin'" round. You see her, tell her come home. I lock her in tonight."

Burt searched the island and tried to look like a nature lover taking a casual walk. His leg ached miserably. Each time he emerged from beneath the trees, he was aware of Hoke watching him from the tower. The longer he walked the more uneasy he became. Mother hen March, he thought wryly; one of your chicks is missing.

He paused to look at cabin four. Could she be in there with Charlie? Surely not of her own free will, in which case she'd be making some noise. The cabin was silent behind the curtained windows. Burt thought of the moan, and of the missing fourth man of the party—

"Sir, you wish to go in?"

Burt whirled and glimpsed the white flash of Maudie's T-shirt inside a clump of bamboo. He looked up and saw that the palm trees which lined the path screened the cabin from the watchtower. He stepped back and watched her crawl from the bamboo.

"You hide well for a big girl," said Burt when she squatted beside him. "What have you been doing?"

"I watch the people pass in the path. You wish to enter one of the cabins? I watch for you."

"No, I was just wondering why one man stays in the cabin all the time."

"I know."

"Why?"

She was gone before he could stop her, then it was too late to call her back without warning the man inside. With frozen nerves he watched her climb the ladder outside the bathroom, her white cotton skirt riding high on her heavy brown thighs. Why had he assumed a sixteen-year-old girl would be clumsy? It was not true in Maudie's case. She moved with the silent efficiency of a burglar, lifting the cover off the water barrel, plunging her hand inside, and drawing out a dripping metal case slightly larger than a cigar box. She replaced the wooden cover on the barrel, climbed down the ladder, and ran across the path. Burt drew her behind the bamboo and took the box. It was surprisingly heavy, with only a hair-line crease revealing where the lid joined the box proper. A combination lock held it shut. It seemed to be made of hard carbon steel; he'd have trouble getting it open even with a cutting torch.

"Who hid it?" he asked.

"Big man who shoot the frigate bird. I see him up on top and ask myself, what he hiding in the water? Later I go see."

Burt shook the box, but it gave no sound. If it held money, it would take huge bills to total the fortune Rolf had mentioned. He doubted that they'd risk putting currency in water. No doubt it would be jewels, perhaps diamonds . . .

"See if you can put it back," he told. Maudie. "No, wait—"

He'd heard the screen door slam on the cabin. Through the screening bamboo he watched a man walk around the corner of the cabin, yawning and hitching his suspenders over the harness of a shoulder holster. The coarse brutal cast of his features duplicated those of Hoke, except that his head was topped by a coarse curly mop of brick-red hair. He stood at the foot of the ladder and looked up. Burt held his breath, then released it slowly as the man walked on around the corner. Burt waited for the sound of the screen door. When it didn't come, he told Maudie to see what he was doing.

She left, moving with a silence possible only for one who had spent all her life on the island. She returned a moment later and whispered: "He stand in front smoking."

Burt cursed silently under his breath.

"You wish to hide the box? I know a place they never find."

Burt frowned. There'd be trouble when they found it missing, but maybe that's what he needed. Make something happen, end the suspense, sow discord among the thieves. If one group thought that another group had stolen the loot, and if Burt could keep his own people out of the way . . .

"Let's go," he told Maudie.

She led him over the low ridge between the cistern and the fumaroles, moving with a speed he found difficult to match with his leg hurting and the box under one arm. Beyond the cistern, she dropped to her hands and knees and started down a green tunnel in the tall, thick grass just barely large enough to sneak through. "Goutis make these path," she said over her shoulder. Burt crawled after the bobbing rump with the white skirt drawn tight over it. He was streaming sweat when they emerged on a steep rocky beach. A grove of stunted guava trees hid them from the man in the tower. Ahead of him Maudie moved along a low cliff, leaping from rock to rock with the agility of a mountain goat. Burt followed, planting his feet carefully on the slippery rocks. He saw her disappear through a crack in a cliff; he squeezed through behind her and found himself in a dark, narrow tunnel. Black water swished around his shoes; ahead, the tunnel disappeared into blackness.

"Now we mus' get wet," she said. She seized his hand, and in total innocence raised her dress to her waist and waded in. He felt the lukewarm water climb to his knees, then to his thighs. Her hand pulled him gently upward; his feet found holes in the rock and he climbed until her hand was withdrawn from his. Burt stood on level ground and sniffed musty air. A match flared, and a kerosene lamp sent probing yellow fingers against the gleaming walls of a tiny cave.

"I come here when *Maman* shout at me," she said. "Only you know now, and me."

Her eyes shone in the yellow light. Burt saw two garish, spangled dresses hanging from a jut of rock; below them lay a foam-rubber mattress and a thick woven blanket stenciled with the words: *S.S. Carlotta, New York City.* On a wooden box sat a ceramic ash tray labeled: *The Mermaid, Charlotte Amalie, St. Croix.* Beside the box were four pairs of women's shoes, a spunglass fishing rod, and an empty Haig-and-Haig pinch bottle. On top was a cigar box full of cheap bracelets and earrings, a half-dozen tubes of lipstick, a totally unnecessary home permanent outfit and, oddest of all, a squeeze-bottle of shaving cream. He felt like laughing; she was like a bower bird, lining her secret nest with glittering objects and understanding none of them.

"Now I understand why you learned to move so quietly," he said.

Her eyes grew round. "You don't tell Miss Joss? I take only what people leave about."

Burt picked up a platinum wedding band and read the engraving: *All my love, J.S.* "I'll bet there's been some hell raised," he said. "But I won't tell."

He tossed the ring back and turned to her. "Now listen, Maudie. I'm going to hide this box near here, but I won't say where. If anybody asks you, you can say truthfully you don't know anything about it. Okay? The men who lost it aren't like the others who come here, they'll kill you to get it. Understand?"

She nodded, her eyes wide.

"Okay, now go home. If there's trouble, shooting, you can come back here. Otherwise don't come near the place. Go."

After she'd gone, Burt gouged a loose stone from the wall of the cave, wedged the box iside, then jammed the rock back in place. It was sunset when he stepped onto the pebble beach. Nature seemed to be making a gesture of defiance after a bleak, gray day. The clouds on the horizon opened like a parting curtain and revealed the sun floating like a huge golden pumpkin on the sea. Streamers of rose-purple light arched overhead and draped the entire island in a glowing net. Burt had a brief stirring insight: all human activities were like the rustling of mice in a magnificent mansion; a man's hunger for diamonds was only a futile effort to capture and hold a fragment of the sun. He felt a brief urge to jump in the sea and swim away, leaving all these people to their own sick objectives.

The urge returned as he reached the path and saw Godfrey running toward him on his bandy legs. He felt a creeping fatigue; he knew he was about to be entangled in a net of other people's problems.

"Sir, you remember the guitar strings you give me?"

"Yes. Why'd you stop gathering wood?"

"Everybody wanting to eat, sir. Boris ask Coco and me to help."

Burt felt anger pinch his nostrils; how did you convince these people that there was danger?

"Well, what about your guitar strings?"

"I hang them behind the bar, now they are gone."

"Did you tell Joss?"

He nodded. "She say tell you. She sick in bed."

Lord, now I've become the island's labor counselor. "I'll try to find them later. Now get Coco and get back to gathering wood. Stay away from the club, you hear?"

The boy nodded and shuffled away.

Burt stopped by and looked in on Joss; she was propped up in bed, looking as though she felt every one of her years. She said she'd just been down to the club and wasn't going back. "It's the weather, Burt, my nerves are shot. That woman's down there throwing it around, and there's nothing but hard looks going back and forth. I've had enough nightclub experience to know there's trouble coming. Well, let them tear up the joint, let them kill each other off with those guns they carry. I couldn't care less."

At the club, Burt found Rolf and Bunny seated at one table. Nearby sat Ace Smith and the red-haired man, both looking totally ludicrous in neckties, starched white shirts, and business suits.

"Get your boat running?" asked Burt as he passed Rolf's table.

Rolf nodded curtly and looked down at his right hand. It lay on the table top, clenching and unclenching.

Ace called out with false joviality. "Hey, bird lover. Have a drink with us?"

"No, thanks," said Burt, stopping beside the table. "You two are a little overdressed for a tropical island."

"Habit," said Ace. "We're used to eating with chicks."

Yeah, thought Burt, noting that the suits were heavily padded and thick in the chest. They'd left their big guns in the cabin, but they wouldn't go out unarmed. Those suits undoubtedly concealed the small artillery.

Burt chose a table nearest the bar and sat down to assess the scene. Boris was carrying drinks, his massive dignity unimpaired by the red-headed man's playful belligerence. He kept shouting for drinks, making the kind of noise a man makes when he's afraid of silence. Ace drank quietly, his small dark eyes roving somewhere in the area between Bunny's collarbone and the bodice of her peasant blouse. Rolf seemed preoccupied, unaware that Bunny was meeting Ace's eyes from time to time, and that little electric messages were crackling between them.

The explosion came with the serving of dinner. The red-haired man demanded food; Boris came out and set a plate of canned beef and crackers in front of him.

"What the hell is this, horse meat?"

"No, sir. Bully beef, sir."

"Take it back and get me a steak."

"I'm sorry. There is nothing else."

"Don't tell me we're paying ten bucks a day for this!"

Boris stood like a soldier at attention, his black face frozen in stoicism.

"You hear me? Is this what we get for ten bucks?" The man was shouting, his face as red as his hair.

"Yes, sir."

"Well, take it!" He threw the plate at Boris, who moved just enough to allow the plate to sail past and land harmlessly on the sand outside. The blob of bully beef, however, struck him on the right side of the face. He stood for an instant without moving while the greasy red meat slid down his cheek and became trapped in his goatee. Then he turned and strode behind the bar. Burt heard the sound of sliding metal; he peered over the bar to see Boris draw out a curved, three-foot cutlass. Burt felt the hair prickle on the back of his neck.

"That's no good, Boris. He's got a gun."

Boris looked at Burt, his smeared face wrinkled up as though he were about to cry.

"I kill him, sir. Got to kill him."

"Wait a minute."

As Burt walked toward the redhead's table, he warned himself to keep cool. But he'd been under pressure too long. The anger boiling inside him had to find an escape. He stood beside the redhead's chair and spoke with tense contempt.

"On your feet, carrot-head. The bartender's waiting for your apology."

The man looked up in surprise. "The hell he is. Well, the day you see Charlie Tate apologize to a goddamn spade, you can—"

Burts actions went suddenly out of his control. His foot kicked out and struck the leg of the other's chair. The big man sprawled backward, his mouth wide with surprise. He landed flat on his back and started clawing at his lapel. It seemed to happen in slow motion; Burt was rocking forward on his feet, preparing to launch a kick at the other's wrist, when he heard a faint swish of air beside his head. The fallen man's features convulsed suddenly, then flowed loose like a bowl of mush. His coat fell back and Burt saw a spreading wetness on the starched white shirt. In the center of the stain, like a pin stuck in the heart of a red, red rose, was a knife buried to the hilt.

Burt turned and saw Rolf zipping up his jacket.

"I should've searched you for a knife," said Burt.

"I told you I didn't like guns." Rolf's eyes held a reptilian glitter; his lips were pulled back from his white teeth. Bunny was staring down at the man, breathing so hard that her bosom swelled above her blouse like a pair of inflated balloons. Ace sat in his chair with his eyes narrowed to slits. No expression crossed the mask of his face, but Burt felt it would take very little to make him draw his gun. Boris leaned over the bar in a hypnotic stare. A particle of dried beef flaked off his cheek and fell to the floor. For the second time that day Burt felt he was involved in a play; soon the curtain would close, the redhead would rise and go off-stage, and they would all gather in the dressing room for a drink.

"Hell." He turned to Rolf. "You didn't have to kill him."

"I know. I could have let him shoot you."

"He wouldn't have killed me. I was about to—"

"Kill him yourself?" asked Rolf with a smile.

"Don't kick a dead horse," said Burt. "We've been through that." He turned to Ace, who seemed to have slumped lower in his chair. "You plan to do anything about this?"

Ace gave a shrug which had no effect on his face. He mumbled, "Charlie was hot-tempered. He shouldn't have gone for his gun. He lost the toss and I guess he paid for it." He gazed up at Rolf with a vague appeal in his eyes. Burt thought of a gorilla caught in a trap. "But life goes on, don't it? What happens now?"

Rolf turned to Burt. "What happens, Burt?"

Here it was, on his back again.

"I'll take the body to St. Vincent, turn it over to the authorities. I'll need your boat." He glared at Rolf, challenging him to bring his game into the open. "You'll have to give them a statement."

Rolf nodded. "I know the rules, Sergeant."

"Sergeant!" Ace blinked at Rolf. "You called him Sergeant."

"He's a detective in a jerkwater Florida town," said Rolf. "No jurisdiction here, of course. But somebody has to take over in an emergency." Rolf gazed out over the lagoon, where the Coleman lantern sent its white light across black water and picked out the plunging spray on the rocks. "We can't go until tomorrow."

"Tomorrow early," said Burt, still puzzled by Rolf's cooperation. "I'll also take Joss and the boys, and Jata and Maudie."

Rolf raised his brows. "Evacuating the island, Burt? Declaring martial law?"

"Just getting them out of the line of fire, Rolf. Any objections?"

"No, it's a good idea. See you in the morning."

EIGHT

Burt didn't even consider trying to sleep. After throwing a blanket over the corpse, he sent Boris up to the tower to keep watch, then sat down at a table to guard the body. Joss tiptoed in a half-hour later to get a fresh bottle. Her eyes were bleared with sleep. She gave a small shriek when she saw the body, but calmed down as Burt told her what had happened.

"I'm surprised at myself," she said, slumping into a chair. "I actually feel relieved. I'm not scared about what's going to happen, because it's already happened."

"Maybe," said Burt.

"I just wonder what it'll do to business. Isn't that crass of me?"

"You'll be snowed under, Joss, by the same kind of people who crowd and push and sweat when you carry a corpse out of an apartment, that gape through the windows of smashed trains and tour auto graveyards to see the blood on seat cushions. Pretty slimy types. You won't like them."

She drummed the table absently with her fingers. "Maybe I'll close up. Wouldn't cost much to live if I didn't try to keep up facilities for guests. You could come whenever you want ... and your wife, if you ever stop being too finicky to give a girl a chance."

She rose suddenly and went behind the bar. She lifted out a bottle and shot him an inquiring look. "Something for your nerves, Burt?"

He shook his head, watching her fill a glass.

"That's right, you don't have any." She tipped the glass and drained it as though it were water and she'd just come off the desert. She filled another glass and carried it back to the table with the bottle. Four drinks later she laid her head on her arms and began snoring. Burt sat and listened to the boom of the surf. The light dimmed; he lifted the Coleman lantern off a nail and pumped it full of air. When he finished, he saw three huge gray rats tearing at the blanket which covered the body. He routed them and saw two more peering over the edge of the platform, twitching their whiskers. He stamped his feet and they disappeared. Another approached the body from the kitchen, moving in a humped shuffle. He launched a kick which sent it scurrying, but there were more squeaks and chitters from the thatched roof overhead. He looked up and saw a half-dozen tails hanging down from the rafters. They know, he thought, the yellow-toothed little bastards know death has come to the island. He lifted down the lantern and set it beside the body. Its upward glow filled the club with weird, looming shadows, but it kept the rats away.

Boris came in, sat down on the bench, and laid the long cutlass across his knees.

"Everybody asleep?" asked Burt.

"All cabins dark, sir. But I think nobody sleep in number three."

"Oh?"

"The woman go there, meet the hairy man outside. Kiss-kiss. Go inside. Lights off. One hour ago."

Burt frowned; he couldn't imagine that Bunny would risk Rolf's displeasure by sneaking off on her own. Maybe Rolf had thrown the woman to Ace to keep him quiet. Bunny was nothing if not adaptable.

"Watch the body," said Burt, rising and stretching. "Don't let him bother you."

Boris smiled thinly and touched the cutlass. "I had no fear when he living. Now he is out of it."

Burt sat in the tower. Across the water came the distant sound of a dog barking idiotically, incessantly. Above him the stars sent down a frantic, coruscating brilliance. Below him the surf was a brilliant white snake which held the island in a triple coil, expanding and contracting. He smelled the sea and felt the rainwashed breeze on his face. He perceived tranquility, but didn't feel it. Something evil was slithering over the island; something worse than the rats, because it wore the body of a man.

"Burt, you up there?"

Burt jumped at the nearness of Rolf's voice. How had the man moved up so quietly?

"There's hardly room for two," said Burt.

"What are you doing—" a soft, breathy grunt, and Rolf was over the parapet and kneeling beside him "—watching the stars?"

Burt kept taut despite the friendly sound of Rolf's voice. Only a yard away lay a five-hundred foot drop to the rocks.

Rolf looked up at the stars and drew a deep breath.

"They *are* beautiful tonight, sort of washed by the rain. Orion, Cassiopeia, the pale disc of Andromeda. We're looking out into time, Burt, six billion years into the past. You know how that makes me feel?" He went on without pausing. "It's all a game, isn't it?"

"Sometimes," admitted Burt. "I feel that I'm also involved in the game, which means bound to follow the rules."

"You play by the rules because you don't trust your own nature."

"Does your master know you're out?"

Rolf laughed. "Satan? I wonder if you aren't right," He chuckled softly, obviously pleased. "I came up to talk, Burt. Killing does that; it enlarges me, intensifies my senses." He leaned forward. "Can't you feel the pygmies down below us? Their petty emotions boiling, their fears? Joss lying asleep in the club with her bottle beside her? Thinking of ... what? Strange whirling shapes and curtain-calls she missed and men she didn't kiss. Old Jata with her door nailed shut against Damballa and a dozen other red-eyed beasts; her daughter twitching beside her, fighting those teen-age chemicals with the brain of an eight-year-old ..."

"How about Ace and Bunny?"

Rolf darted him an oblique look. "Sleeping the sleep

of satiety, I suppose." He paused. "I shouldn't be surprised that you know. You have your own spy network, haven't you?"

Burt grunted. "I thought you had her under better control. You disappoint me."

"And you disappoint me for not understanding. Weren't you watching Ace at dinner? Of course you were. Jumpy, scared . . . wanting. There's a close correlation between fear and the sex urge. Look at wartime illegitimacy—"

"So you threw him Bunny."

"He'd have grabbed her anyway. Islands have that effect on people, Burt. You tend to think of direct solutions to your problems. Look at Joss. She wants a man, she makes a blunt physical appeal. If that doesn't work, she offers booze, free meals, a pad. She uses what she has. Ace there. He's a man of violence. Lives by the gun. He wants a woman, he'll take her. A man gets in his way, kill him. Simple and very effective . . . on an island. Who'd have defended her? You, March?"

Burt sighed; he was tired of Rolf.

"It's all hypothetical."

"Sure, because I didn't allow it to become real. Now Ace will awaken in a tranquil state, a little less afraid—"

"What's he afraid of?"

"Of you, now that he knows you're a cop. You represent society, and in his eyes that makes you bigger than you really are." He laughed softly. "It also makes him more dangerous to you, since Ace destroys what he fears."

"I suppose everyone tries—"

"I don't."

"What are you afraid of?"

"Everything." Rolf laughed without humor. "And therefore nothing. Hostility surrounds me; there is nowhere to run. And so I don't run."

"And your wife? What's she afraid of?"

Rolf looked narrowly at Burt. "You're very interested in Tracy. I wonder why." When Burt said nothing,

Rolf went on in a musing manner. "Actually, I don't know what Tracy's afraid of. Something, certainly, but I can't pin it down. I've never been able to reach her, which is why—" He broke off, then went on in an abrupt, businesslike voice: "I have to know if you're with me. Tonight."

Burt felt his stomach tighten; he'd been expecting the question. "If I say yes, how will you be sure of me?"

"'You'll be given a job to do. Kill Ace."

Burt caught his breath then let it out slowly. "Why?"

Rolf ignored the question. "You could do it your way. Get him cornered, box him in, taunt him until he makes a try at you. Then you cool him. Self-defense; I've seen other cops do it." He laughed shortly. "You can't lose, March. Neither of us can."

Burt forced down his anger; he wanted to learn more. "I want to know the rest of the deal. All of it."

Rolf was silent a moment, then sighed. "All right. Briefly. It started with a *mordida*, a bribe. A cabinet minister in a small Latin-American country—you'll excuse me if I slip the specifics—was getting rich on pay-offs from foreign firms who wanted to do business there. I paid—several times—and I got to know him. He lived austerely by *politico* standards, only one mistress, one Cadillac, one mansion. What did he do with the money? I was curious, and I told Bunny to find out. But then came the revolution, the insurgents won concessions from the government, among which was the purge of the corrupt minister. He made a run for it and got himself cut down by machine-gun fire. Bunny had learned only one thing; the country's ambassador to the U.S. was his closest friend. The ambassador also got caught in the purge, but he claimed asylum and holed up in a beach villa on Florida's east coast. Bunny and I returned to the States, where she met the ambassador and—in the direct manner of hers—quickly insinuated herself into his favor. It took her a year to learn his secret; not an easy year, either. The man was a greasy troll with the manners of a swamp rat. The minister had been converting his loot into diamonds

and sending them to the ambassador in sealed diplomat-
ic pouches. The diamonds were now in a strongbox
locked in a safe in the villa. I had already begun build-
ing my organization. You may appreciate the way it
was done, March. I went to a sleazy part of Miami,
pretended to be rolling drunk, and flashed a few big
bills. As I expected, three men followed and cornered
me in a doorway. I'll never forget the surprised look on
their faces when they realized that their victim had become an assailant. You see, I too had learned that one
may kill legally in self-defense. I have left more than
one unidentified body in alleys for the police to find. I
killed one, leaving Hoke and Charlie alive. They were
frightened, and since fear is the seed of loyalty—perhaps the only way to insure the loyalty of such men—I
decided to use them. They led me to Ace Smith, who
had just finished an eight-year sentence for armed robbery. I wanted to make the theft look like an ordinary
burglary, you see, so that they'd never connect it with
me. And to shorten the tale, I now have nearly a mil-
lion dollars in diamonds."

"Converting ice to cash is no easy trick."

Rolf sighed. "March, this is my magnum opus, my
greatest creation. Nothing is left to chance. Tomorrow
night I shall meet two men from the ambassador's
country. They will give me two hundred and fifty thousand dollars in U.S. currency. I return the loot to its
rightful owners—it's all arranged."

Burt grunted. "Even the disappearance of Ace and
Hoke."

"Of course. That's why I chose this island. They expect the split to be made here. It will be, but only between you and me."

"What about Bunny and your wife?"

Rolf made an impatient gesture with his hand.
"You've asked enough questions, Burt. Are you with
me—or against me?"

Burt suddenly felt the weight of two sleepless nights.
He shook his head tiredly. "Rolf, you didn't read me
well—"

"I read you. We could have made a natural team, if only you'd lost a few illusions." He rose to his feet. "I'd like to give you more time, but you're beginning to distract me . . ."

Burt was startled to see the glint of the gun appear suddenly in Rolf's hand. Irrelevantly, he said, "I thought you didn't like guns."

"I don't. They're too impersonal. But sometimes there's no choice."

Burt felt his stomach cringe; the gun was pointed directly at his belt buckle. He talked quickly to gain time, watching for an opening.

"You have a choice, Rolf. Killing the man in the club can be called self-defense; stealing the ambassador's jewels could probably be fixed, since they were obtained illegally in the first place. No need to add murder to your crimes."

Rolf laughed softly. "Burt, I was saving the news until you were committed to my side. Bunny killed the ambassador as she left his bed and board. There's a nationwide alarm from the FBI on down. One more murder won't matter—"

A scream split the night air. Burt lunged and jammed his shoulder into Rolf's stomach. The gun exploded and spat a yellow tongue of flame which burned Burt's cheek. Rolf fell back against the ledge; the ancient mortar crumbled. Rolf teetered a moment, then disappeared.

The scream came again and again; the senseless ululation of a woman in terror. Burt left the tower and ran downhill, falling once in a headlong dive, peeling the skin off one forearm. He reached the club as the screaming changed to a low, sobbing moan. He saw Joss staring at the bench. There sat Boris with his whispy goatee on his chest, his eyes half-closed, staring at the floor with a morose, pensive expression. But he was neither morose nor pensive; he was dead. The cutlass had been swung with tremendous force, lopping off his right arm at the elbow and penetrating three inches into his side. The redhead's body was gone.

"Burt . . . Oh, Burt. Look, I woke up and I . . . I . . ."

She was suddenly sick on the floor. Burt saw Godfrey and Coco standing white-eyed beside the bar.

"Coco, you and Godfrey run up the hill and start a signal fire. We'll need—"

"Hold it. Nobody leaves."

Burt turned to see Ace holding the over-under gun. Hoke stood beside him with the shotgun resting on the railing.

"Let's have your gun, bird lover. Lay it on the floor and step back." When Burt hesitated, Ace said: "These shotguns throw a helluva shower of lead. If we didn't get you we'd get the lady or one of the niggers."

Burt did as he was ordered; Ace came forward, picked up the gun, and shoved it in his pocket. He jerked his head toward the body of Boris. "His own fault he got it. I thought I hit him hard enough to lay him out for a hour. But he woke up and jumped me." Ace touched a purple swelling above his eye. "I had to kill him. I was told to get rid of the body without being seen."

"Rolf's orders?" asked Burt.

Ace gave a twisted smile. "Did you think Bunny was running it?" He stepped back to the railing. "All right. Everybody on the floor, flat on your backs with hands above your head."

Everyone obeyed except Burt. Ace jabbed the gun in his direction. "You too, birdman. You ain't privileged."

"How do you know I'm not?"

Ace glared at Burt, then called over his shoulder. "Hoke, go find the boss. I wanta know what he wants done with this character."

"Kill him," said a voice from the darkness.

A second later Rolf stepped into the club. His clothes were torn. Blood ran from a long cut across his forehead and dripped from dirt-crusted eyebrows. He was holding his right forearm in his left hand, and Burt saw that his wrist was impossibly twisted. His mouth was open, his lips drawn back so tightly that a white rim showed around them. Each perfect white tooth had an outline of blood, and his eyes held a remote, glassy look. It was obvious that Rolf had lost the hard glaze of self-control.

"Did you hear me? I said *kill him!*"

Ace lifted the rifle. "Sure. You mean, right here?"

"Didn't I say—? No, wait." Rolf strode to the body of Boris and jerked out the cutlass. It made a soft sucking sound. Joss moaned and closed her eyes.

Burt backed away as Rolf approached. Why didn't those idiots run, Coco and Godfrey? No, they had to lie and gape like a pair of fools and Joss was out cold—

His back struck the bar just as Rolf swung the cutlass high over his head with his left hand. Burt leaped aside and the cutlass buried itself in the mahogany rim. Rolf tugged at it frantically with one hand. He seemed crazed with pain, half-sobbing the words: "—I gave you a chance, I tried to be friends, I asked you to come in with me—"

"Rolf, listen—"

He raised the cutlass again. "—you tried to kill me, broke my arm—"

"—and hid your diamonds!"

Crash! The cutlass gouged a two-foot splinter from the bar. Ace ran up and seized Rolf's arm. "Boss, listen! Listen to what he said!"

Rolf shook free, started to swing again, then stopped and gazed around the room as though he'd just awakened from a long sleep. He blinked at Ace. "What?"

"He said something about the diamonds."

Rolf looked at Burt. He was breathing heavily, but the glaze was gone from his eyes. "You found them?"

"And stashed them again. If you kill me you'll never find them."

"Hoke, go check the barrel." The big man left, and Rolf tossed the cutlass to the floor. "Cover these people, Ace, especially him." He walked over to Godfrey and jammed a toe in his ribs. "Get me a pan of water and a cloth."

The boy scrambled toward the kitchen. Rolf slumped in a chair and passed a shaky hand across his forehead. He moved his wrist slightly and went pale.

"Broken, I think. I'll have Bunny splint it."

Godfrey brought the water and stood holding it with hands which trembled so violently that the water rippled and splashed. Burt felt dismay as he watched Rolf calmly wash the blood and dirt from his face. The others had missed their chance; now Rolf was once again in control of himself.

"I'm glad you stopped me, March. That isn't my scene, to kill in anger. I must have lost my head while I was wedged in that crevice below the tower." He rinsed out the cloth and watched the water turn a dirty brown. "I like to talk to a man, learn how his mind works, learn some of his background. Then when I kill, I am he. I am both victim and killer. Maybe I have a drive toward suicide, since I tend to identify with the victim. Fortunately my survival drive is stronger—"

Hoke clomped onto the plank floor of the club. "The box ain't there."

Rolf closed his eyes, then looked at Burt. "You're spoiling my time-table, and this makes me angry. Better tell where it is."

"I'll mail you a postcard from the States."

Rolf smiled thinly. "That earns you a few more hours of life, Burt. But you won't enjoy them." He waved at Ace. "Take him to cabin two. Then wake up Bunny. She'll enjoy this bit."

Burt walked ahead, listening to the footsteps of Ace and Rolf behind him. They were away from the club now, entering the deep velvet shadow beneath the palms. Burt took a deep breath, then took off in a low crouch. He heard Rolf shouting behind him: "Don't shoot! Don't shoot!" He veered off into the low bush between the cabins, saw a white shape loom in front of him. He tried to sheer off, but his weak leg buckled and he crashed against the figure. He heard Bunny's high squeal of surprise, then they were both on the ground and Burt was entangled in perfumed limbs, trying to fight free of her beach coat. Something struck him behind the ear, so heavy and solid that he knew, in his last moment of awareness, that he'd been clubbed by a shotgun butt.

NINE

"Take off his shirt, Bunny."

Rolf's voice dipped into the well of unconsciousness and drew Burt upward. He felt fingers clutching at his shirt like a tiny trembling animal. He caught the aroma of perfume and another heavy, musty odor. His chest was laid bare and caressed by the quick moist breath of the woman. Her fingertips left damp tingling tracks on his flesh and he could smell the high electric tang of her sweat. She was trembling, excited at this approaching opportunity to mortify a man's flesh. Her nails raked his shoulders needlessly as she pulled the shirt from beneath him; he heard the voiced exhalation from her nostrils and felt his stomach harden.

"I think," said Rolf musingly, "that I will let Ace begin."

"But he ain't awake."

"He'll wake up when you begin."

Still Burt kept his eyes closed. A spot of warmth touched his stomach, then pain gouged his nerves and ripped a blazing path to his heart. His eyes flew open; he saw Ace with sweat beading his forehead, bending over him with a lighted cigarette. Bunny knelt on the other side, her lips slightly open. She was bent forward at the waist, pressing her palms to her stomach as though in pain. Rolf sat in a chair and looked down at Burt through half-closed lids. His taped wrist hung from a sling around his neck.

"What did you do with her?" asked Burt.

Rolf raised his brows. "Typical cop. With his first breath, lying flat on his back, he begins the interrogation." He paused. "Do with whom?"

"With your wife."

"You've got a problem, haven't you, Burt? Can't you get my wife off your mind? Okay, let's trade information. I'll tell you where she is, and you tell me where the diamonds are."

Burt shook his head, and Rolf waved his hand at Ace. "Go on. Who told you to stop?"

Again came the fiery jolt of pain, and it took all Burt's energy to keep from crying out. He sent out the tendrils of his thought, gathered up a thousand red-hot needles of pain and drew them up into his brain. He compressed them into a ball and probed it, gauged it, rolled it around, felt it loosen up and flow through his mind with a syrupy sweetness. His fingertips went hot and tingling, as though they were shooting off electricity. The room rippled in the yellow lamplight, then resolved itself into a pattern of glowing lines. The lines dissolved and flowed into a redness so brilliant it hurt his brain; the redness became purple, then green, blue and yellow, as though a series of colored silk veils were being drawn across his eyes. He felt himself sinking into a sweet, warm bath. He was a mind and no more; his body was cold unfeeling clay.

Rolf's voice reached down again:

"I envy you, Burt. I don't fear death, but pain drives me insane. How can you ignore it?"

Burt fought to avoid returning, but the act of fighting defeated him. His chest felt as though a thousand burning splinters were stuck into it. The concrete floor beneath his bare back was slick and cold with his sweat.

"You don't . . . ignore it," he gasped. "You . . . change it."

"Interesting," Rolf mused. "Hold on a second, Ace. I've got an idea. Bunny, go get that overgrown adolescent, the daughter of the cleaning woman."

Burt tried to sit up, but his hands were bound above his head and anchored to something immovable. His feet were stretched wide apart and tied to the bedposts. He was trussed up like Gulliver in Lilliput. He lay back amid a fresh outpouring of sweat.

"What . . . do you want with her?"

Rolf smiled at him. "Obviously pain isn't your weakness. But you have another vulnerable point; you're emotionally hung up with other people." Rolf laughed. "That's a weakness I don't have. Go on, Bunny."

The woman sighed and rose from her knees. "You've hardly started with him."

"He won't talk, Bunny. Keeping quiet is his life insurance."

"Can't Ace go?"

"Go, dammit! You won't miss anything."

When the door closed behind her, Rolf waved to Ace. "Light another cigarette."

Ace frowned. "I don't get it. You said—"

"I said he wouldn't talk. From March I want something else."

"This is crazy," grumbled Ace as he lit a new cigarette off the old one. "What else can you get out of him?"

"He knows. Don't you, Burt?"

The pain came again, and through a mist of shifting colors, Burt thought: Sure I know. You want to hear me yell and plead. But when I do you'll lose interest in me; you'll be disappointed because another person had turned out to be weak and controllable. And you'll go on looking until you find a man who's stronger than you, and you'll say to him what you've been saying to everybody else. Kill me if you can. And you'll be relieved as hell when it finally happens. . .

The pain was gone, and Burt heard Rolf repeating his question. "You know what I want, Burt?"

Burt said, "You want to make me mad."

"Oh, very good, And why?"

"So . . . so I'll try to kill you." He tugged at the ropes. "Turn me loose and I'll give you a show."

"Not yet, March. You'd mark me, and I have to meet some people tonight. After that . . . there's nothing I enjoy more than a fight to the death."

Burt curled his lip. "You and a lot of other people.

As long as there's some guarantee it won't be your death."

"I can guarantee that myself," said Rolf.

"You . . . you're disgusting, Rolf. You strip yourself of ten thousand years' civilization and call yourself a higher being. You're a throwback; your only advantage is that other people are civilized. In a primitive society the tribe would've stoned you to death."

"Or made me king," said Rolf quietly. "Let's leave off the cigarettes, Ace. The smell of burning flesh is beginning to annoy me."

Ace sat back on his haunches. "I watched him in the club while I waited to snatch Charlie's body. Rats drive him nuts."

"Do they?" Rolf eyed Burt a moment, then shook his head. "No, it would require too much apparatus; a live, starving rat and a metal box. Besides, the idea of using animals to torture men offends me somehow. Only man has earned that privilege—"

A scream of pain cut him off. Burt stiffened, then realized it was a man's voice. The scream came again; faded to a low sobbing moan. Rolf looked at Ace and jerked his head toward the door. "Get him quiet."

After Ace had gone, Burt said, "Charlie's nightmare is still around, it seems."

Rolf frowned. "Another hitch in the plan, I'm afraid. We had a young man driving the car. He caught a bullet from one of the ambassador's bodyguards."

Ace came in panting. "He's out of his head, boss. I found him outside; he didn't know he was on an island. He was gonna give himself up and get a doctor to look at him." Ace shrugged. "He pulled the bandage off and got the blood going again. I don't think he'll make it through the day."

Rolf chewed his lip a moment, then stood up. "Stay with March. I'll see if I can help the kid."

Ace sat on the bed and smoked in short, nervous puffs. Burt watched him, reflecting that Bunny had been gone a long time. He hoped Maudie had followed orders and gone to the cave.

Ace got up and walked to the window. He stared out at the blackness.

"Worried about the murder rap, Ace?"

Ace whirled. "Why should I be? Bunny—"

"Sure, she killed the ambassador. But if you're caught, she'll say it was you, and you'll burn. Nobody believes an ex-con."

"Nobody's gonna get caught. Rolf is smart."

"Smart, yes, but he's not normal, Ace. He doesn't figure profit and loss like you and me. He's got his own balance sheet, and you don't know what's on it."

"I know there's two hundred and fifty grand on it. That's enough."

"Maybe that's what Charlie thought, too. He didn't expect a knife in the chest."

"Ahh, shut up." Ace turned back to the window, showing Burt his massive back.

"Why did you think Rolf picked this island to make the split? One by one he'll cut down the percentages. First Charlie, then Hoke or the kid there—"

Ace whirled, his face twisted. "Shut up! I told you—"

Bunny opened the door and looked around. "Where's Rolf?"

"With the kid. What about the girl?"

"Couldn't find her. The old lady said she took off during the excitement. She wouldn't unbar the door, but I peeked in and saw she was alone. I'll go tell Rolf—"

"Stay with gabby. I'll go."

Bunny sat on the bed and lit a cigarette. After a minute she stood up and nudged Burt's arm with a slippered foot. "Want a drag, baby?"

Burt gazed up the twin white columns of her legs, past the short revealing beach coat, and saw the teasing half-smile on her face. "No, thanks."

"Come on, settle your nerves." She squatted down and brought the cigarette toward his mouth. At the last minute she reversed it and jammed the glowing tip between his lips. Burt felt the lash of pain and spat out the burning sparks.

"You hate all men, don't you, Bunny? Is that why you killed the ambassador?"

"Him! I killed him because he was a pig." She moved out of sight behind his head. "If you're curious, I'll tell you how it happened. Ace and the boys were coming in at ten, see? I was supposed to keep the old guy busy. At nine-fifty he was watching TV, and I came up behind him like this." Burt felt her fingers stroking his hair. "I rubbed his greasy old bald head, I kissed him like this—" moist lips touched Burt's forehead "—then I did this—" Burt shivered as she blew in his ear "—then this—" Burt stiffened at the touch of cold metal against his temple. "And I went . . . BANG!"

Burt jumped. Bunny threw herself on the bed and whooped with laughter.

"You're as crazy as Rolf," he said.

She sat up and brushed the hair from her eyes. "Sure. That's why we make a good team."

"I've seen your type before, Bunny. You hang yourself up with a destructive man knowing damn well that he'll wind up destroying you, too. What motivates you? You want to die?"

She opened her mouth to answer, but Ace came in and slumped down on the bed. His face was greenish-white. "Jesus!" He shook his head slowly. "I went over there." He swallowed. "Rolf is talking to the kid like a father. Telling him everything's gonna be all right, that he's gonna take care of him. And all the time he's got this little thin wire, running it through his fingers, and . . . you know what he's gonna do?" Apparently Ace had his limits.

Burt felt his stomach twist. When had Godfrey's guitar strings disappeared? Yesterday afternoon. Then Rolf had planned something like this. . .

Bunny jumped up and started toward the door. Ace caught her arm and threw her across the bed. "He doesn't want you."

Bunny bounced up, her eyes blazing. "Don't get any macho ideas from last night. I take orders from only one man."

Ace shrugged. "So go over. But he'll throw you out. He said he wanted to be alone."

Bunny sighed and lay back on the bed. She looked at the ceiling and sighed. "Men," she breathed in disgust.

Minutes passed. Ace jumped up and paced the room. He jammed his fist into his palm. "I don't understand the guy. Why does he drag it out?"

"I told you why," said Burt.

Ace took a step toward him. "I warned you, fuzz—"

He stopped as the door opened. Rolf walked in with a light step, his eyes bright. He pointed a finger at Ace and jerked his thumb toward the door. "Weight him down and put him in the launch with Charlie. I'll dump them both at the same time."

Ace merely stared, and Rolf added: "If you see Hoke, tell him the kid died from loss of blood. He would've anyway."

Ace nodded and went out, walking like a somnambulist. Rolf lowered himself into a chair and closed his eyes; he seemed calm and sated, like a lion who has just devoured a heavy meal.

"The girl is obviously hiding out," he mused. "She grew up on the island, she could stay hidden for hours. I could bring in one of the others, but that would take time. I've got to leave here in an hour." He stood up and walked to the window. "Those manchineel trees; I've heard that their sap does violent things to a man's eyesight."

Burt had an idea; he moaned softly. "You ... wouldn't blind a man."

Rolf looked down at him and scratched his chin. "I wonder if I've found another weakness."

"Going blind is a hard knock for a detective," said Bunny.

"Hmmm. Yes." Rolf reached inside his shirt and

pulled out a knife. He held it out to Bunny, hilt first. "You'll have to slash the bark to get it."

Bunny went out with a flash light and returned five minutes later with a medicine bottle full of milky fluid. They knelt beside Burt, one on each side.

"Hold his left eye open," said Rolf.

Cool fingers pried his twitching lids apart; Burt looked up into an emerald green eye with an iris splintered with gray. Her pupil was half-dilated, but he knew she wasn't drugged. She didn't need drugs. . .

Rolf held a medicine dropper above his eye. Burt stared at the glistening globule which appeared at its tip, saw it tremble and fall—

Ahhhh!

There was no need to pretend pain. It burned like acid. Burt thought of the old island doctor who'd told him the blindness was temporary, not much worse than poison ivy; he writhed and struggled and recalled that the old doc had been drunk when he said it.

"A last chance, Burt. You can save one eye." Rolf paused, then: "Okay, Bunny. Hold it, there. . ."

The pain was worse this time, double. Burt squeezed his eyes shut and stared into a fiery redness like the pit of a volcano. Molten rock spurted up and lashed his brain. Ah, but something else was down there, cool and black. He groped downward with all his being, entered the blackness. *Peac*e. He curled up and went to sleep.

TEN

He awoke in terror. For an instant he thought he really was blind; there was nothing but blackness outside his eyes; it stopped his vision not in front of his eyes but at their surfaces, as though his eyeballs had been painted black. Then he made out the details of the window; just a paler shade of black against the total darkness of the room. He was puzzled. There should have been a sunrise. Then he heard the soft susurration on the thatched roof. It was raining; a heavy, windless rain, as though the clouds were not releasing moisture but rather leaking.

He lay still for a moment trying to sum up the situation. He was still tied. Maudie, presumably, hidden. Boris dead. Jata, locked in. Joss, Coco and Godfrey, totally harmless. He hoped Rolf realized that. Unfortunately, he was a psychopathic killer and capable of killing everybody on the island.

He heard soft breathing above him; occasionally there came a rustle of bedclothes and a soft high moan. Female. He was in the keeping of Bunny, and Bunny was a restless sleeper.

He waited until the wind rattled the palm leaves outside, then he tested his bonds. Tight. His hands were tied to some protuberance on the wall. He moved them and found a mortar seam jutting out between the stones. He rubbed the rope against it and the concrete crumbled damply. Damn Joss for using lousy cement. . . .

He settled back and breathed heavily through his open mouth. He wished he'd been left with Ace instead of Bunny. There was no way to reach the woman.

Something tickled his wrists, and he felt a shooting

113

pain in his hand. A rat, hell. Lie still:oh, if I only had something to put on my ropes so the rat would chew them. . . .

This is the rat that gnawed the rope.

But no, he's moving up, pitter-patter of little feet heavy weight on chest, he smells the blood from those burns . . .

No!

It was more than he could take; with a thrusting twist of his body he rolled over, spilling the rat on the floor. It scurried away, and from above him came the crackle of the coconut straw mattress. Her voice came sharp and clear without a semblance of sleepiness:

"Fuzz, you awake?"

Burt said nothing.

Patter of bare feet, scrape of a match, tinkle of lamp chimney. Yellow light filled the room. Careful not to blink, Burt stared at the ceiling. He heard the whisper of her bare feet, saw her face appear only inches from his. Her hair was a black, tousled cloud.

"You're awake, sure. You're really blind, are you? Rolf thought you might fake it."

Burt tightened his lips and kept staring upward. The strain made his eyes water.

"You crying, Burt? No, you wouldn't cry, would you? What have you been doing?"

"Counting sheep, what else?"

She laughed without humor. "Can you count what you can't see?" She tugged at his bonds with a skillful hand, then rose to her feet. "You should've talked sooner. You wouldn't have had to spend your last hours as a blind man."

She picked up the lamp and walked toward the bathroom. From the corner of his eyes, Burt saw the curved outline of her body silhouetted by the lamp she carried before her. Her black, ankle-length gown flowed around her like smoke.

The door closed, leaving the room in half-darkness. Burt closed his eyes and felt the tears course down his temples, into his ears. He heard the gurgle of the chain-flush toilet, then the sputter of the shower. Outside the day grew lighter.

The bathroom door opened. Burt turned his head back toward the ceiling. He was aware of the woman walking toward him on silent bare feet. She moved in a slow, stagy, hip-rolling fashion, shrugging the gown off her shoulders and catching it behind her. A moment later she stood over him, filling his vision with the twin hemispheres of her breasts bisected by the gentler curve of her stomach. She bent down, and he smelled the soap-washed odor of her skin. He felt her hand searching intimately.

She rose with an abrupt snort. "Man, you *are* blind. Blind as a bat."

She walked away and Burt heard her rummaging in her suitcase.

She appeared again in his field of vision, laid her clothing out on the bed, and began dressing. Without looking at her directly, Burt noted the difference in the way a woman dresses in the presence of a man, and the way she does it when she's unaware of being watched. There was no languor of movement; buttons and zippers were no longer keys which could open windows into a mysterious world, but only garment fastenings. It was a matter-of-fact operation, totally devoid of erotic ritual, like harnessing a horse or setting a table. Her voice filled the spaces between the swish and rustle of her clothing. She would accompany Rolf to meet the men in Caracas, she said. Rolf wanted her along because she knew the language better than he did. She talked to Burt with a vague condescension, as though she had already come to regard him as less than a man. Burt decided that it would be worth all the pain in his eyes, if it only made her careless. . . .

"Where is Rolf now?" he asked.

"He went to Petit—" She caught herself. "He went to give his wife her . . . . uh, food for the day. He's picking me up on his way back. Then we'll . . ."

Burt barely heard the rest of it. Petit, he thought, Petit Martinique, Petit Baliceaux, Petit Mustique, Petit

Cannouan, Petit St. Vincent, Petit this and that. Even the Tobago Cays had three islands with such a prefix; Petit Rameau, Petit Bateau, and Petit Tabac. One of those remote clods, he decided, but which one?

He turned his attention to the woman. Dressed now in a white blouse, smoke-blue skirt and matching shoes, she sat on the bed and peered into a hand-mirror propped against the lamp. Her words became slurred as she applied lipstick:

". . . spend two days without me, Baby, but don't break up. I'll be back. Meantime you'll be tied up here in the dark like a little rabbit. No food, no water. Don't try to untie yourself because Hoke or Ace will be outside. They can't come in because I'm padlocking the door and taking the key. Don't bother to yell because they won't answer. Rolf calls it the black hole treatment; you're supposed to gabble like a turkey when you come out. I don't know, personally; I did two years in a reformatory because of guys like you and we went through things just about as bad. But maybe Rolf knows what he's doing . . ."

Rolf did know what he was doing, thought Burt; so had the Chinese Reds, the Japanese and the wardens of Devil's Island. They'd learned that you totally destroy a man's will when you bury him alive.

He watched her reach into her purse and take out a tiny black cylinder not more than a half-inch long. She spread a handkerchief on the table, unscrewed the cylinder, and took out an object which glistened like a drop of water on her right index finger. With her left hand she spread the lids of her right eye and touched the finger to it. Her eyelids fluttered rapidly. She clenched her fists and beat them gently against the table.

"Oh, brother, I know how you felt when Rolf dropped that sap in your eyes. These lenses are a bitch at first, like running around with a cinder in your eye." She pulled out a tissue and blew her nose, then bent to insert the other lens. "But I can take it another week."

"Oh, is that when you drop the masquerade?"

"That's when they stop hurting." She gave a laugh

which ended in a sniffle. "Man, you live in a dream world. This is no masquerade, this is for real. Bunny DeVore is dead; I'm Tracy Keener for the rest of my life."

Burt felt his lips go dry. "And the real one? She dies, I suppose."

"You've got the scene, Baby." Bunny closed her purse, got up and went into the bathroom. Her voice floated back through the open door. "It's been a drag running out to . . . to that island every day, practicing how she moves, how she walks and talks. Rolf's a real perfectionist. What if we meet some of our old friends, he says. Personally, I don't intend to give them the time of day, I'll be in and out of Capri, Monaco, Hawaii, and anyway there's my height. But Rolf says a woman's height is expected to fluctuate according to what shoes she's wearing and—"

"When?" asked Burt.

"When what? Oh, her. Just as soon as we get back. I've got her down cold."

Cold. The word echoed in his mind.

Bunny returned with the two-piece plastic shower curtain. She wrapped it repeatedly around his wrists and ankles, making a separate knot with each loop. Burt wondered where she'd become so skilled at tying a prisoner.

She stiffened at the sound of the launch. "There's Rolf. So long, Baby."

She bent over him, her hair brushing his cheek. Her lips touched his with brief, surprising tenderness. Her lipstick tasted of mint. She raised her head and he saw her eyes glistening. "That's so you'll remember me. And . . . this!"

He saw her arm move, but he forced himself not to flinch. Just before the hand struck his face, it curved into five bright red claws which tore furrows from his ear to his nose. Then she was gone.

Time became a succession of half-heard sounds: The heavy clump of Hoke's feet, Ace's softer tread, the scratch of a match and the whisper of rain on palm

leaves. The rain ended; the sun came out and converted
all moisture into steam. The walls of the unventilated
room became beaded with moisture; breathing was like
trying to inhale warm, damp cotton. A rust-colored,
eight-inch centipede crawled onto Burt's right leg,
nosed around his trouser cuff while Burt held his
breath, then dropped off and disappeared through a
crack in the wall.

Burt felt a tingle of excitement when he heard Ace
and Hoke in mumbled conversation on the porch
veranda; perhaps the seed had sprouted and borne
fruit. He was certain when he heard the splintering
crack of wood and the protesting screech of metal. The
door crashed open and Ace walked in.

"You wanta tell us where the diamonds are?"

"What do I get out of it?"

"You live. We're getting out of here before Rolf
comes back."

"How?"

"That's our problem." He snapped his fingers, and
his voice showed the strain of his decision. "C'mon.
Make up your mind."

"I'll show you," said Burt. "I can't tell you."

They untied him and led him outside. Burt forced
himself not to blink, though the light was blinding after
the darkness of the room.

"You'll have to lead me," he said. "It's near the fumaroles."

"What's that?"

"Where the water shoots up from the ground."

"Yeah, this way." Ace caught the protruding end of
his belt and pulled him roughly through the tangle of
vines around the cabin. "Okay. We're on the path
now." Burt found it easier to fake blindness if he stared
straight ahead with his eyes unfocused. He bumped
once into a palm tree and another time sprawled forward with his feet tangled in railroad vines. Hoke guf-
fawed behind him; this was the kind of humor he could
understand.

Short, salt-crusted grass crunched beneath his feet.

He let himself be pulled along and felt the strength flow back into his aching muscles. He sensed Hoke behind him with the shotgun ready. He knew his life would be measured in minutes if he showed them the diamonds; killing him would be a reflex action not worth debating.

"Okay," said Ace. "Where is it?"

Burt stood two yards from the ten-foot cliff and felt the spray cooling his face. He tried to remember exactly where he and Coco had found a half-submerged cavern two years ago. Giant langouste liked to hole up there during the day, and they had taken out dozens.

He dropped to his hands and knees. "There's a hole here somewhere."

"Here's one!" shouted Hoke.

"Okay, stick your hand in. It's out of sight under the edge."

Hoke laid his gun on the grass beside him and plunged his arm in up to the elbow. Ace watched him, his attention off Burt for an instant. Burt took two running steps and dived off the cliff. He struck the hissing water and clawed for the bottom. The water was clouded with foam and sand particles. He groped along the cliff, fighting against the water which tried to thrust him to the surface. He found a hole and pulled himself inside. He swam into darkness, his lungs bursting, aware that he could be entering a blind pocket. Above him was solid rock. He visualized himself trapped beyond the point of no return, drowning with his head pressed against the roof of the cavern. Then his hand groped into air. He surfaced and filled his lungs with great gulps. He found a narrow shelf where he could stand with his head above water, and began the long wait. No sound reached him except the gurgle of water and the hiss of air. There was no light; no measure of time except the steady rise and fall of the waterline on his chest and the changing pressure on his eardrums. After a time even that became unconscious, like the rhythmic beat of his heart.

It could have been two hours or three when he de-

tected a faint glow coming through the water from the
entrance to the pocket. He watched, his mind suspended, until the glow faded and disappeared. Night-time
now. He couldn't be sure that someone wasn't waiting
at the edge of the cliff, but there was no way to make
sure. He dived down and pulled himself blindly
through the tunnel. He felt the force of the surf and
came to the surface. The gibbous moon in the east
seemed brilliant as day after the darkness. The black
silhouette of the cliff was unmarred by any manlike
shape. The sea seemed unusually calm, and there was
no wind. He moved northward along the cliff, swimming silently without raising his arms from the water.
He emerged on the pebble beach, found the crevice,
and groped toward Maudie's cave. He saw the yellow
glow of lamplight before he entered.

Maudie lay curled up on the foam-rubber cushion,
dressed in a green silk dress with red chiffon bordering
the neckline. Burt knelt down and shook her plump
shoulder. Her eyelids fluttered, then opened wide. She
sat up, her features swollen from sleep, then pressed
her palms against her forehead and brushed the hair off
her temples.

"You don't seem glad to see me." said Burt.

"Yes, but . . ." She indicated her dress and sighed. "I
wish to change before you come."

He frowned. "You expected me?"

She nodded. "They say you walk blind into the sea
and drown, but I know—"

"You've been out?"

"Yes, but nobody see. Godfrey meet me and give me
these." She pointed at a case of bully beef and several
cans of ship's biscuits. "They watch the others, but they
never see me."

The sight of the food made Burt aware of the growling complaint of his stomach. He began to open a can
of the bully beef but Maudie jumped up. "You sit, sir.
I will serve you."

Another time Burt might have been amused to see

this young girl playing hostess in a gaudy dress too small for her burgeoning body, while yellow lamplight flickered on the walls of the cave. She apologized that he had to eat with a strip of shingle; she gave him water from the Haig-and-Haig pinch bottle, then squatted before him and stared with intense fascination while he ate. Gradually he extracted from her the details of what had been happening on the island.

Rolf and the woman had gone, a fact Burt already knew. Joss and the boys had been told only that Burt was a prisoner, and that if any of them misbehaved he would be killed. That had kept them quiet until Coco and Godfrey had been pressed into diving for his body. When they failed to find it, Ace had decided that he'd been carried out to sea. Joss had then been taken to her house and locked in, replacing Burt as a hostage. One of the men guarded her all the time.

Burt thought it over; apparently the two had given up their scheme to get the diamonds, and settled down to wait for Rolf's return. This posed a dilemma for Burt: should he try to sneak up, overpower the two men and . . . then what? He had to get Tracy Keener out of Rolf's way. (He had decided she must be on one of the Tobago Cays, ten miles away.) Her death seemed a foregone conclusion when Rolf returned; that of Joss and the boys remained problematical. If he tied Ace and Hoke, then went after the woman, they might get free and kill the others out of sheer vengeance. The best thing was to leave the island as it was, let the two men think him dead so they wouldn't get nervous, get the woman to safety and come sneaking back with reinforcements.

"Maudie," he said. "Do you know where Joss keeps the skin-diving equipment? The tanks, masks, fins, that stuff?"

She nodded. "In the room beside where the boys sleep. You wish me to bring it?"

"Can you get it without being seen?"

"Truly." She rose, seized the dress at the hem and

pulled it over her head. She stood in the bra and a pair of men's shorts knotted around the waist. "Nobody see me at night when I wear no clothing."

Burt wondered if he'd ever get used to the way women had lately disrobed in his presence as though he were a bronze Buddha. He watched her untie the shorts, drop them to the floor, then kneel with her back to him. "Will you help? I do not understand the hook."

As Burt unhooked the clasp, he asked: "Can you carry the stuff? Those tanks are heavy."

"I am more strong than Coco," she said. "He learn this one night when he catch me in the path." She shrugged off the bra and walked to the cave entrance. She turned, invisible except for her teeth and eyes. "You sleep. I bring everything."

Burt lay down on the cushion and tried to visualize a map of the Grenadines. Mayero was the nearest populated island to the Tobago Cays; he vaguely remembered a tiny, African-like cluster of thatched huts. He would leave the island at dawn, invisible beneath the water, swim to Mayero, leave his tanks there as a deposit on a rowboat. He'd row across the long stretch of open sea to the Tobago Cays, pick up Tracy Keener if she was there, and . . .

Maudie's hands shook him awake. "Sir, will you look?"

He raised his hands and saw the equipment lined up for his inspection. Tanks, carrying frame, fins, mask, belt of weights, knife—

"You forgot the regulator."

"What is that?" Her naked body was wet and glistening like an otter's pelt.

"A round thing on a black hose. Goes in your mouth."

"I get it," she said, and left.

This time he did not wake up when she returned. He dreamed that he was swimming and encountering a black-backed porpoise in the water. He was wrestling the porpoise, trying to push it beneath him, when he

woke up and looked down into the wide white eyes of
Maudie. She lay passive in his arms, using none of her
boasted strength.

He rolled onto his back. "Sleep on the other side of
the cave, Maudie. I've got a long swim tomorrow."

ELEVEN

He rowed across the silent, oily sea. Behind him lay
the main cluster of the Tobago Cays, four islands so
close together that men could converse from one to the
other and hardly raise their voices. He had searched all
four without finding any sign of her; only some im-
mense turtle shells where fishermen had long ago
stopped for a feast. Now he rowed toward one lonely
island a mile or so from the others. The fisherman in
Mayero had called it Petit Tabac; it looked odd with a
single palm tree growing from the low bush-covered
mound in the center. He decided to land on the sand
spit which curved out at the western end. Gray rocks bit
through the surf around it, but the sea was calm
enough to land without danger. He was thankful for
the calm sea, with reservations, for it was a heavy,
threatening quietness. And so hot. He took one hand
off the oars and touched the soft blisters on his nose.
The man on Mayero had said: "Hurricane comin'."
And Burt had said: "I've been hearing that since I
came to the islands. When will it come?" "Today," said
the man, and in that matter-of-fact way the islanders
talk of death, had added: "You will die on the sea."

Now Burt could see the black cloud like a low ob-
sidian cliff on the eastern horizon. He would have been
thankful for rain—just a little. The sun was a white-hot
rivet tacked to a blue-steel sheet of sky. Sweat made his
palms slick on the oars and complicated the task of
working the boat in through the rocks. He reached the
line of low breakers and leaped out, seized the prow of
the boat and dragged it up the steeply sloping beach.
Damn, they made these things heavy. Not more than
six feet long, and it must weigh a hundred pounds. It

124

took all his strength to drag it ten feet above the surf-line. He reached beneath the thwart and took out an oilskin bag containing a tin of biscuits and two cans of bully beef. He tied it to his belt beside the plastic-handled fish-knife, then climbed up the slithering sand to the top of the mound.

The entire island was less than a quarter-mile long. It formed a narrow crescent which began where he stood and dwindled to a line of rocks on the eastern end. There the pelicans sat hunched over, like movie-goers waiting in the rain. He saw two structures of black rock, shaped like Navajo hogans. It was the only shelter on the island; she would be there if anywhere.

He jumped and slapped his ankle, saw the blood trickle down from the bite of a sandfly. He started down the beach. A gust of wind tore the breath from his lungs, stung his face with sand, and then was gone. He looked to the east and was appalled to see how the cloud had grown while he was beaching his boat. Now it covered the lower quarter of the eastern sky, black as approaching night. It was laced with red and yellow veinings of lightning, like mace on nutmeg. He felt a chill of foreboding and looked at his boat lying vulnerable on the sand. He ran back, uncoiled the heavy line and tied it to a jutting boulder. Then he ran back down the beach, his canvas sneakers slapping against the hard-packed sand.

She sat with her back against one of the stone shelters, her head sunk on her chest, her eyes fixed on her hands lying palm up across her thighs. Burt stared in frozen shock, his triumph at finding her wiped out by the appalling sight of her condition. The tangled mass of her hair was bleached a pale orange on top, hiding her face except for the peeling tip of her sun-blistered nose. Her long-sleeved denim shirt was open at the neck; the skin beneath it was welted by mosquito bites. Her long flannel slacks, once white, were now a stained, spotted gray. Her legs were stretched out before her, widespread, with the cuffs pulled up to her calves. Above her dirty white socks, her ankles were raw and bleeding from the bites of sandflies.

"Tracy Keener," he said.

She didn't look up. Beside her he saw the biscuit tin which he decided must contain her supplies. On the sand lay an open untouched can of beef, its contents dried and green and covered with flies. On a plastic bag lay a needle, its tip stained the color of rust. He knew why she didn't answer; she had just hit herself, and was now taking that first wild soaring ride which addicts call the flash. He knelt and raised her head.

"Tracy. I've come to take you off the island."

She gave him a glazed, unfocused look. "In a minute, baby. You're new, aren't you? Did Rolf come?"

So . . . she thought he was Rolf's man. He decided not to tell her he was taking her away from Rolf; the tie between an addict and the supplier was umbilical.

"Your husband couldn't make it. Come on. Let's go."

"In . . . in a minute."

"We can't wait. Look."

He held her chin and turned her face toward the east. The cloud was growing visible, sending blunt stubby fingers into the sky above them. Even the birds had grown strangely quiet.

"Pretty," she said. "What is it?"

"That's a storm. A bad one." He spoke as though explaining to a child. "We've got to get off before it hits. This island isn't more than twenty feet high. We're going to one of the higher islands. Understand?"

"Uh-huh." She smiled dreamily. "I like your voice."

"Oh, hell!" He seized her wrist and pulled her to her feet. Her legs were like wet spaghetti; she crumpled to the sand like an empty pair of overalls. He lifted her in his arms and carried her up the beach. She draped her arm around his neck and hummed as they went along, keeping time to his footsteps in loose sand. Her lightness surprised him; the skin slid over her ribs, and he felt the hard ridge of her spine beneath his arms.

"Haven't you been eating?" he asked.

"I bet Rolf told you to ask that. Eat, Tracy. I can't have everybody knowing my wife's a hypo. Eating is like putting a tongue depressor in my mouth." She giggled softly and laid her head on his shoulder. "I get everything I need through the skin—Oh!" She stiffened. "Put me down."

"We're halfway there."

"But I forgot my outfit! I can't leave it!"

Her back arched and her thin body twisted in his arms. Rather than hurt her, he loosened his grip and let her fall on the sand. She was halfway running when she touched ground; she was off like a rabbit, leaving him with the sleeve which had ripped from the shoulder seam. She ran with surprising speed against the wind, into the clouds which roiled up before her like black smoke from a refinery fire. Her shirt flapped straight out from beneath her armpits; each rib and each joint of her spine showed starkly white, as though the skin and flesh had been stripped away to leave her skeleton bare. His pursuit was slowed by his greater bulk; he sank deeply into the sand, and the rising blasts of wind stopped him like a brick wall, only to dissolve and leave him staggering forward until he hit another blast.

He reached the stone shelters as she was tucking in her shirt. The plastic bag formed a pregnant bulge above her belt.

"You pulled me down off the high," she said with faint sullenness. "I can walk now."

Going back was easy; the wind hammered against their backs like a giant fist. Surf boiled up around their knees until they had to climb the steep beach and walk in the prickly bush which grew at the center of the island. Above their heads the wind plucked a leaf from the palm tree and flicked it far out to sea.

Burt stopped when he saw the sand spit where he'd left his boat. The sea charged in from both sides, crushing together at the center and raising his boat high on a bubbling geyser of foam, rolling it over and over like a medicine ball on the feet of an athlete, then leaving it half-careened and filled with water. He turned and saw that Tracy had sat down in the sand and was gazing up at the flying debris.

"Can you climb a tree?" he shouted against the wind.

"Of course," she said serenely. "But I don't want to."

"You've got to! We can't get off the——!"

He stopped, for suddenly his voice rang out into absolute stillness. He looked around, and in the weird green light he saw a sight which made him doubt his vision. The island seemed to be slowly rising from the sea. Water poured off their little mound of land, cascading over the rocks, forming little torrents and whirlpools, twisting through acres of barnacled coral. He saw fish left gasping on the sand; he saw a manta ray as big as a barn roof stranded in six inches of water, its huge wings flapping like those of an enormous black moth dying from DDT. He saw a hundred crayfish scurrying between the rocks, frantically seeking the water which had left them; he saw a hundred mounded acres of rock veiled with dripping seaweed, studded with elkhorn and mushroom coral.

In the instant that his eyes encompassed the spectacle of the ocean floor exposed to the hostile air, he saw the reason for it. The sea was leaving the island, sucked up into the blackness which thundered toward them with a sound like a thousand horses drinking at once; coming in like a huge black whale which drank the ocean dry as it came. Burt stood for an instant frozen in a fear so great it was almost ecstasy.

Then he was picking her up and carrying her to the palm tree, ignoring the thorns which tore at his legs. He propped her against the tree, but she slid down, her body limp and boneless. He jammed his knee into her stomach and held her there while his hands tore at her belt buckle. . . .

Her hands fought him feebly. "Hey, what——?"

"I'm going to strap you to the tree with your belt."

She giggled. "But my pants will fall."

"That's not the worst thing that can happen." He jerked her belt from the loops. The slacks sagged to her hips and caught there. He removed his own belt and joined the two, then passed them around the tree and fastened them around her stomach. He pulled it so tight that her rib cage bulged out above it.

"I can't breathe!" she gasped.

He looked down and saw the bewilderment in her dark brown eyes. She didn't understand what was happening.

"Shut up," he said, his voice roughened by a sudden protective emotion. He peeled off his shirt, wrapped it around the oilskin bundle of food, and tied it to the strap which held her.

While he worked, he was aware of the light getting dimmer, like a lamp turned down, changing from yellow to green, and then to blue. Suddenly it became a deep purple twilight. He was gasping for air, pulling it into his lungs and finding it hot and with a strange electric taste. He looked toward the east, out past the tongue of naked dripping rock, and saw the heaving, oily swell of the tidal wave. It seemed to be growing larger as it came, rising higher and higher until he had to look up to see its crest. He could hear it, like an approaching locomotive, crashing over those two flimsy stone huts as though they were matchboxes . . .

He leaped for the tree and wrapped his arms around it. He pressed his face to the tree just as the water struck. His face ground into the rough palm trunk. He tried to gasp but there was no air, only water which had become a lashing monster wrapped around them. It was like being shut up in a tank with a frenzied whale. His feet left the ground and stretched out behind him. His arms popped in their sockets and he laced his fingers, willing them to grow together and never part, even though his arms might be ripped from his shoulders . . .

Then the water was gone, driven on by the wind. The wind was a demon of fury bent on his destruction; it peeled his eyelids apart and hammered his eyes into his skull; it rammed its fingers up his nostrils and jammed a fist down his throat, collapsing his lungs and bloating his stomach. Above him, the palm fronds were stripped away like dandelion fluff blown by a child. He bent his head and pressed it against the tree; he could feel the fibers straining in the wood and hoped it would hold; he wondered how Tracy was, but he couldn't see her. The darkness was total. The rain struck in smothering sheets like wet flapping canvas; the water rushed over the mound and tore at his waist. He felt the sand eroding beneath him, sinking him lower and lower, and he had a sudden fear that their tree might be gouged out by the roots after having withstood the terrible force of the tidal wave. He wrapped his legs around the tree, pried one hand free, and groped around the trunk. His heart sank as his hand touched nothing. He groped downward and touched her naked back; the shirt had been torn away and she was slumped forward hanging from the belts. He seized her hair and pulled her back against the tree. His hand touched her lips and felt them moving. He extended his embrace to include her, feeling the small softness of her breasts beneath his arms.

And then he ceased to think. Time is your enemy, he told himself; to endure you must become a creature without continuity in time, you are a May fly existing on the razor's edge of the instant. Eternity is now; the next breath and the next heartbeat will be another man's problem. Don't let the fingers slip, don't let Tracy's head sag . . . don't think. The world has turned feral; all the elements are united against you, but don't think about that. There'll be no punishment if you survive or don't; all fear of the future is meaningless, for this is Hell . . .

He had no idea how long it lasted, but a sudden peace descended like a cotton blanket. The blackness surrounded them; it was like standing in a huge silo with a tiny skylight far above. Burt looked around in the unearthly, yellow green twilight. They stood on an almost barren ridge of rock laced with tiny pockets of sand. The silence was broken only by the gurgle of runoff water and the slopping of fish trapped on the land. He saw why their tree had remained intact; it was rooted in a pocket of earth in the solid rock.

He felt Tracy move under his hands. "Please, you're hurting . . ."

It was slow work, for his joints had locked together and each uncoupling was agony. When she was free, she straightened and breathed deeply. All that remained of her shirt was the collar and a tattered strip of cloth on the right side. Suddenly she gasped and began to tear at the belt.

"Don't," he said. "We're not through yet."

She kept tugging, and he crawled around the tree and seized her wrists. "Stay put, Tracy! We're just in the center. There's another jolt coming just like the last one."

She looked at him in terror. "But it's gone! My kit is gone. I had it right here—" She pressed her palm to the sunken cavity of her stomach. "I've got to find it! Help me look!"

"*Look*?" He waved his arm. "Where would you look? It's five miles at sea by now."

She looked around, dazed, as though she had just realized that there had been a hurricane. Then she squeezed her eyes shut and screamed up at the tiny circle of light. *"Rolf! Rolf! Where are you?"*

He seized her and shook her until her jaw wobbled, and then she collapsed against his chest and called Rolf's name in a weak and plaintive voice. Her utter dependence on Rolf angered him.

"How heavy was your habit?"

"I'm not sure." Her voice was muffled against his chest. "I used to hold it down to one capsule a day, but then Rolf didn't seem to care, so I gradually took more and more. When you have it laid on you like that, you cabaret all the time. I used . . . maybe three, four a day. Maybe five, I don't know."

"You poor nitwit." Burt was appalled; a person with a habit that heavy could die if left suddenly without it. He'd known it to happen in small back-country jails: The addict thrown into a cell and left to kick the drug cold-turkey . . . convulsions, incessant vomiting, muscle spasms so strong they can throw joints out of place. Eventually the heart bursts, the lungs rupture . . .

He looked down into her eyes, saw the opaque film which, it was said, an addict never loses. Behind that, he saw fear . . . and dependence.

"I'll die . . . won't I?"

She wanted reassurance, and he wanted to give it. He remembered the letters and realized that the prospect of doing without the drug could start her down that same blind alley. He also remembered that he had been unable to see his boat on the sand spit, and that they might be a long time in leaving the island.

"We must get to St. Vincent tomorrow," he lied. "I know a doctor there . . ."

When the next blow struck, he covered her with his body. Hours passed with the wind clawing at his back and from time to time the woman stirred against him. He felt a futile anger at the turn of events. Even if he brought her alive through this, she'd have another hell to go through tomorrow.

TWELVE

The wind died gradually from about midnight on. Burt loosened Tracy's belt and arranged her in a sitting posture with her back to the tree. She moaned but didn't awaken. Burt sat beside her and dozed.

Dawn came with a bleak gray light. The leaden sky was mottled by black clouds kicked along by blasts of wind. Rain drops stung his face like BBs. He looked at Tracy sleeping with her head back, her lips parted. His eyes followed the straight white column of her neck down to her wasted body; the small cuplike breasts were bare and rainwashed to an ivory whiteness. He could see the blue veinings beneath her skin, and he wondered what had given her such a frail, unearthly beauty. Her face seemed to glow with its own cold light; her eyes were shadowed and deep in their sockets. Camille, he thought, or St. Joan of Arc in the dying ecstasy of her martyrdom.

He took off his tattered shirt and put it around her. He stood up and surveyed the debris which had been deposited on their barren rock: Several palm leaves, dozens of coconuts, an entire guava tree stripped clean of bark and leaves, a few shattered boards and assorted specimens of dying undersea life, including a ray the size of a dining room table which was draped over a rock and beginning to swell. He saw that their island had been split in two; thirty yards west of their tree was a twenty-foot chasm of rushing white water. Where the sand spit had been, a few jagged rocks thrust up from the lashing foam. So much for the boat . . .

He draped palm leaves over the trunk of the guava tree and laid Tracy beneath the waist-high shelter. Her forehead was cold and clammy, but she was breathing.

He decided not to awaken her; when the withdrawal pains came there would be no rest for her anyway. He used his knife to open a can of beef and ate half of it with his fingers. He punctured a coconut, drank the sweet water, then gathered up all the coconuts he could find and piled them beside the shelter. At least they'd have no drinking problem . . .

He returned with his last load to find her struggling to sit up. "Lie down," he said.

"But I need my—oh!" She lay back and looked up at him from wide frightened eyes. "I . . . didn't really lose my kit, did I? That wasn't real."

"Yes," he said. "You lost it."

She closed her eyes and began to tremble. He touched his hand to her forehead; it was cold and moist, like the flesh of a dead chicken. Her teeth clattered.

"How do you feel?" he asked.

"Like . . . like th-th-they were squirting hot w-w-water up my n-n-nose." She started to sneeze, then rolled over on her side and retched. Burt sat helplessly until she finished.

"Maybe if you ate," he said.

He handed her the remaining half-can of beef. The beef dropped off her shaking fingers and down the front of her shirt. Her mouth was loose and drooling, and moisture ran out of her nose. He took the can from her hand. "Lean back and try to relax. I'll feed you."

It was a bizarre and intimate scene; he dipped the beef from the can and she ate it from his fingers. He remembered that some Indian marriage ceremony included a ritual of bride and groom feeding each other by hand. He wondered why he should get ideas like that. When the can was empty, he said, "I'll open a coconut. You can drink."

"I . . . I don't think—" Her face turned green. He jerked back just in time to escape the spew of bully beef. She doubled over and vomited again, then again, until all the beef was gone. Still the retching continued. He put his palm on her arched back and felt the spasm rip through her body. He lost track of time and lost count of her convulsions. He saw that there was really such a thing as black bile, and he wondered how much punishment the frail body could stand. He didn't leave her, though there was nothing he could do to ease her pain; he had a strange feeling that soon she would be nothing but empty skin, lying on the sand like a discarded laundry bag.

At last she sighed and lay back. Her face looked like a skull. Cold moisture gleamed on her pale skin. "The doctor . . ." she gasped, closing her eyes. "We've got to go . . ."

"I am afraid—" he began, but he saw the slow rise and fall of her bosom beneath the sweat-soaked shirt. She was asleep; she seemed to be resting.

He rose on aching limbs and walked to the break in the island. Peering beyond, he saw his rope tied to a rock where the sand spit had been. His heart stopped when he saw the rope go taut, then slacken. Could there be a boat on the end of that? It seemed impossible.

He started across the channel where it seemed shallowest. The current slammed against him and tore his feet from the porous rock. He made a leap, seized a jut of rock, and pulled himself to dry land. He lay for a moment panting, then rose and walked to the rope. During the ebb of a wave, he saw the boat wedged between two rocks and filled with sand. He found a broken counch shell and descended, using the shell flange to scoop out the sand. He worked in waist-deep water, scraping his hands raw. Twice he managed to empty the boat, and twice the burgeoning surf drove him to high ground while the boat filled again with sand. At last he managed to drag the boat up above the booming surf. A close inspection showed him that it was far from seaworthy. One hole he could have shoved his head through, a half-dozen others would have admitted his hand, and there were innumerable cracks and pits. He felt no grief; it was a boat, and he had despaired even of that. . . .

Suddenly he heard a shout. He turned to see Tracy standing on the other side of the break, her face twisted in terror. He caught only a few of her words.

"Don't . . . leave me!"

He tried to shout that he wouldn't, but his words were lost in the booming surf. He started running when she stepped into the water. When he reached the break she was a swirling patch of hair twenty feet out. He plunged in and swam with all his strength, caught her by the hair and started dragging her back. It took all his remaining energy, for he had to make a wide circle to avoid the rip current which now flowed through the island. He reached land, collapsed and lay panting, his body limp against the sand. When he raised his head, she was sitting beside him, regarding him with concern in her red, swollen eyes. He spoke with a tired, futile anger:

"How many times do I have to save your stupid life?"

"I thought . . . you were going to leave."

"I was just checking the damage on the boat. Did you think you could swim that channel?"

"No. I can't swim."

He stared at her, speechless. She passed a shaky hand over her face, as though brushing away cobwebs. "Can we go now? I feel as if spiders were crawling all over me."

He rose to his feet. "I've got to fix the boat first. You're on this side of the river now, so the swim wasn't all wasted."

Using the boat's rope to make a handline across the break, he transferred the food, some coconuts, and the most usable pieces of wood. He rebuilt the shelter and began whittling out repairs for the boat. Occasionally a pale sun shone between the clouds. Birds shrieked in the water and fought over dead fish. Two hundred yards out a long gray body left the water and crashed down again, leaving a memory of flashing teeth and streaming blood. Shark-fight, he thought; blood crazed scavengers divvying up some dead monster of the deep.

Better make sure the boat was good, he decided; there'd be small chance of surviving if it swamped.

He fitted a board in place and saw a new problem. The boat would make water like a sieve if he didn't calk the seams. He stood up and searched his pitiful pile of scrap lumber. One fragment of ship planking yielded scarcely enough tar to dirty his fingernails. Beneath his feet he saw a round, black globule. He picked it up and found it soft and sticky, with the sulphurous smell of crude oil. He looked around and saw the beach sprinkled with the globules. Hmm, an oil tanker must have gone down nearby. Well, their misfortune is our salvation. . . . He dropped to his hands and knees and began harvesting the globules.

"'Can I help?"

He looked up and saw her body streaked with the long red marks of her nails. Her hair was an impossible tangle. "Go back and lie down."

"I can't . . . sit still," she said, dropping down beside him. "I feel itchy where I can't scratch. It's in my bones."

He set his teeth and rose. Maybe work would help, there was nothing else he could offer her. "Okay, gather up all this tar. I'll get back to work."

Back at the boat, he started fitting boards in place and cramming in the tar. He half-forgot the woman until he heard her moan. He jumped up and found her lying on the other side of the shelter, the little pile of tar beside her. She was arched backward, her heels nearly touching the back of her head. He knelt beside her and asked her what was the matter, but she could say nothing, her lips were pulled back from her teeth, her eyes rolled back into her head. Muscle spasm, he thought. He placed his hand against her back and found the skin tight as stretched canvas. The muscles on her legs stood out like ropes; the veins on her head were like worms. Her face turned blue, then black; Burt stuck his fingers into her throat to free her tongue; he put a piece of driftwood between her teeth to keep

her from biting it in two, then began kneading and probing her muscles.

Gradually the spasm ended. She straightened and lay
gasping, her legs kicking fitfully like those of a dog
which has just been shot. "I . . . never kicked the habit
before," she gasped. "How . . . long does it last?"

Burt had no direct information, but he'd heard that
it lasted anywhere from two days to a week. He
couldn't tell her that. "You're over the worst part," he
said. "From now on it gets easier."

He carried her to the shelter and returned to the
boat. The convulsions came again a half-hour later. He
massaged her until she relaxed, and by then it was
dark. He ate, but she could not touch food. Her lips
hung slack and moisture ran down her chin. He lay beside her all night, stroking her body when the convulsions tore her apart. He came to regard her as a piece
of his own flesh, like an arm or leg. He felt her cramps
as though they were his own; he agonized when the
pain tore her apart. He could only relax when she did,
and that was rare. Toward dawn he napped, only to
awaken and find her gone. He sat up and saw her
down beside the water stepping out of her slacks. Her
nude body was tinged with a halo of pink from the rising sun. He ran and caught her before she got her
knees wet. She gave no struggle as he carried her back
to the shelter; her eyes were vacant and there seemed to
be nothing behind them. She was limp and boneless as
he put on her clothes; dressing her was like dressing a
doll. When he finished she half-opened her eyes.

"You're all right now?" he asked.

"Yes."

"You don't really want to die, do you?"

"Yes."

"Oh, now look." He spoke as though instructing a
child. "Death is something you don't ask for, Tracy.
It'll come, that's in front. Maybe it's a kick, who
knows, but it's the very last one you'll ever get. Making
it happen is like going out at noon and praying for

night. Night will come, it's all arranged. You don't
have to push it . . ."

He broke off, for she had closed her eyes. He rose,
vaguely disappointed, for he had wanted to ask why
she'd taken off her clothes before she attempted suicide.
So many women did. He'd always wondered . . .

He ate and got to work on the boat. He checked her
frequently to see if she was dead. She never was, and it
never stopped surprising him. She didn't sleep, just
seemed to drift away for a time. He decided that she
must have tremendous inner strength. Others had
kicked it cold-turkey, but most of them had been nour-
ished and cared for. This was the rawest, roughest
setup. He wondered how Rolf had enslaved her.

At three that afternoon she said she was hungry. She
was too weak to eat, and Burt fed her again from his
fingers.

"I feel that I have died," she said. "Maybe I'll live
again, I don't know. It seems like a lot of trouble."

"You don't have to make the same mistakes."

"Oh, but the hunger is in me. Every little nerve is
going gabble-gabble-gabble, we want it we want it we
want it." She closed her eyes. "When I go back to Rolf
he'll be able to get it, and I can't put it down. . . ."

"You won't be going back to Rolf," he said, but she
was asleep.

He worked until dark, then lay down beside her.
Late that night she awoke trembling.

"Put your arms around me," she said. "Keep me
warm."

He did, and her hair tickled his nose. He didn't
move for fear of disturbing her. He thought she was
asleep, but then she said:

"My blood is like ice-water. This . . . is in the way."
He felt her hand between them, pulling apart the shirt.
Then her cool bare flesh rested against him, pressing
hard as though she were trying to curl up inside his
body. He felt her relax and sigh.

"What's your name?"

"Burt."

"That's a very . . , abrupt name. Are you an abrupt man? No, you're not. You're very calm, in a deep sort of way. Rolf is calm only on the surface. I can't understand why you work for him."

"I don't."

She stiffened. "But you said—"

"A lie," he said, then he told her about finding her purse with the heroin, the discovery of the masquerade, and the entire chain of events which had led him to this island. "I've wondered about one thing," he said when he finished. "Did you know what was going on?"

"Oh, part of it. I knew there was something crooked. I knew that woman was posing as me, because she came out with Rolf and gawked at me. But then I thought, what the hell, maybe she'll make a better Tracy Keener than I did. You realize I wasn't really here. My body was just something you stuck a needle into. It was a chemical substance, I mixed it with dope and became real. When it wasn't mixed, I was nothing."

"You were something," he said. "Before you got hooked."

"A child. An unformed creature. You wouldn't be interested."

"I would, yes." He looked up and saw the purple dawn lacing the sky. "Right now I've got work to do."

The boat was nearly ready; Burt had saved the two best boards for oars. He ate and started work. She watched for a few minutes then said:

"I feel I could help."

"Okay, start cramming tar into the cracks."

While she worked she told him what she'd been before she got hooked: intelligent, only child of respectable parents, the kind of background that makes you feel smarter than you really are. She'd left home to seek the usual things: romance, independence, and a broadening of experience. Working for Rolf seemed to offer it all; he took long trips and would no doubt leave her in charge. Eventually she too might taste the glamour of foreign travel. But he told her nothing, and she became frustrated. Once she tried to open a forbidden filing cabinet. It burned, filling the office with acrid smoke. At first Rolf was furious, but then he cooled. "I should have warned you. If you try to open the cabinets incorrectly, it triggers an incendiary which destroys the contents." She asked, "But why? What part of your business has to be hidden?" He took her out to dinner that night and explained: The art objects were hidden in the ground; he was bringing them to a public which could appreciate them. Technically illegal, perhaps, but so was drinking on Sunday. Burt, having heard Rolf's warped and faultless logic, believed Tracy when she said she'd been confused. What confused her still more was that Rolf took an abrupt personal interest in her. He found her an apartment near the office at a rental she couldn't resist. He took her out to dinner and on boating trips. Gradually she lost touch with boys she dated and girls she'd known.

"I understand it now," she said. "He'd taken me into his confidence; now he had to take control of me. I remember the night I realized Rolf had taken over management of my life. We were eating at a restaurant overlooking the sea. I felt the kind of panic you get when an elevator sticks between floors. I told him I was quitting my job, and he nodded as though he had been just about to suggest it himself. You could never get ahead of Rolf. Then he said: 'I've decided to get married, Tracy. Why don't you think it over?' Well, you know the cool impersonal way he talks, as though he'd just recognized the need for a wife in the abstract, a need which had nothing to do with me. When I realized he was proposing, I looked down at my lobster and waited for the wave of joy which is supposed to hit you at this time. When it didn't come, I told myself I was a fool for not taking a rich handsome man when he was in an offering mood. Still I don't remember thinking it over or saying, yes, I'll marry you Rolf. Suddenly one day I was standing in front of a stranger with a Bible in his hand, and there was Rolf beside me. I ran." She laughed. "The minister's wife ran after me.

All girls felt that way, she said. Ten years from now I would laugh and wonder how I could have been so foolish. So I thought, well, you've got to play the rules, Tracy, marry this man and be blushing and happy. So I went back in and the ritual came off. I didn't even have to think; they told me every move to make. If it wasn't set up that way there'd be a lot fewer marriages. What they need now is some ritual to carry you through the wedding night."

She was silent, looking down at her tar-blackened fingers. "I don't even like to think about it."

"Don't."

"Why not?" She squinted at him. "How could I keep secrets from you? You've fed me, dressed me ... I've been like a baby just being born. This is another bit of the old Tracy. So I'll tell it and get rid of it."

But she fell silent again. He put one finished oar aside and was starting another when she spoke again:

"He brought a bottle up to the room and fixed me drink after drink. He never touched it. I poured it down, my nerves stretched tight, getting sorrier every minute about what I'd done. And Rolf watched me with that faint smile, until finally I asked with a little laugh: 'Well ... don't we go to bed or something?' He laughed too and said: 'You don't want to.' And I said, 'But I do, certainly I do,' even though he was right, as he usually is. Then we got into this unbearable discussion of whether I wanted to or not, and I began to wish I hadn't drunk anything, because he was twisting my words, making me say things I didn't want to say. And finally I shouted: 'What am I supposed to do?' And he said, 'If you wanted to, you wouldn't have to ask.' I left him and went out to a bar, and drank more liquor until I was just sober enough to fall into a taxi and give my address. Then I sort of dozed off, half-aware that we had pulled off the road, and the taxidriver was getting in the back. Suddenly the door opened and there was Rolf. I just remember his white teeth shining and his grunts of violence, then the driver was slumped down between the seats, unconscious. And then Rolf

... while the cars whizzed past on the highway and the driver gurgled through his broken mouth ... Rolf consummated our marriage." She looked down for a moment. "Before I came out of my daze, Rolf took me off to Nassau and treated me like a queen for two weeks. I'm ... susceptible to that sort of thing. When we got back, we got into another fight about a trip he was making, and taking that woman along. I knew about her. And ... it happened again. Only with a guy in a bar; Rolf came in when he was trying to buy me a drink and cut him to pieces without even mussing his hair. And then ... home again. I began to realize he couldn't make love without fighting first—"

"He is crazy, didn't you know that?"

"I thought so. But he talked so logically. You try to tell him and he winds up proving you're the one who's crazy. Arguing with him is like firing bullets against a rock; he catches all your words and throws them back at you. And the bottle was always there, for me ..."

"How'd he get you on the needle?"

"Oh, a bad hangover. He gave me some white powder to sniff. It was ... wonderful. I'd been taking it for about a week and thought it was some fantastic new headache powder—don't laugh, I was stupid, I know that. I started complaining about it burning my nose, and he brought home a needle. Then I knew it was heroin. I threw a scene, I told him no, no, no, and he just smiled and said, "Well, I'll leave this here in case you need it. I didn't want it. But then I learned for the first time that nobody wants it. You need it, like food. Somebody mentions it and your insides light up. Your mind says, take it away, and your body says *gimme, gimme, gimme*. So ... I got hooked. Rolf was finally in complete control. He kept me supplied and ignored me. I didn't care; all my troubles were soft fluffy things I could blow away like dandelion seed." She looked up in sudden fright. "I've lost the last four years, Burt. Can I ever get them back?"

He shook his head. "What's gone is gone, but there are more years to come."

"And what if I see Rolf and he says, 'Here's some stuff, baby, in case you want to get straight?' "

"We'll have to make sure you don't meet him." Burt held up the finished paddle. "Ready to go?"

"As ready as I'll ever be."

THIRTEEN

Tracy bailed with half of a coconut shell while Burt rowed. He was heading north, but the current pulled him inexorably south into the open sea. The handmade oars twisted in his palms; they were blistered and bleeding when Tracy looked up and shouted:

"Look!"

Burt turned to see a schooner bearing down on them. A moment later O'Ryan leaned out of the wheelhouse and beamed down. "Man, they tell me on Mayero you crazy. I sail over to get the body."

In the wheelhouse five minutes later, O'Ryan produced a quart of black rum. He looked at Tracy shivering beside Burt and trying not to choke on her rum. "She look nothing like when I see her first."

"She's been through a hurricane out in the open."

"Eh—eh. That was a bad one. Many people die." He told about a fishing village on St. Vincent which had been destroyed by the storm. Flooding rivers had cascaded down out of the mountains, swept the shingle huts into the sea and buried the site in twelve feet of silt. A hundred bodies had been recovered and the digging continued. O'Ryan then passed from the tragic to the commonplace without changing his tone; Joss's island seemed to have suffered little damage, he said; a few palms had blown over and half the roof of the beach club was gone. He was sure nobody was hurt, otherwise Joss would have signaled him in.

"You saw her?"

"Yes. She come out on the beach and waved me off."

Burt frowned, then he understood. No doubt Ace had watched from hiding while he held a gun on Coco or Godfrey or one of the others. Rolf's men knew how to get the most out of hostages.

"Was there a launch in the lagoon?"

"No."

Ah, thought Burt, then Rolf's return had been delayed. There might be a chance to bag the whole crew.

People stared as they walked down the cobbled waterfront street of Kingstown, St. Vincent. O'Ryan had loaned Burt a shirt which was far too big for him, and had produced a gaudy dress with red polka dots which hung from Tracy's shoulders like a laundry bag. She stumbled beside him, and Burt saw the gleam of perspiration on her pale face.

"Is it coming again?"

"A . . . little."

He watched her carefully as he said: "The doctor isn't too far from here—"

"Don't say it." She seized his hand in a painful grip. "I'm too near the edge. Stay with me, don't let me out of your sight. Please. You're my backbone."

The sergeant raised his brows as they stepped into the police station. He was a tall, thin blue-black Negro, dressed in a white jacket, black shorts, and white knee socks. Burt read in his eyes the temptation to eject such a disreputable looking pair, then the second thought that these people were white tourists, and that nothing could be lost in giving them quiet and respectful attention. He offered them chairs, introduced himself as Sergeant George, and fingered the buckle of his leather crossbelt while Burt talked. When Burt finished, he said:

"You're a detective sergeant?"

"Yes. I don't have my badge—"

Sergeant George waved his hand. "It wouldn't have any standing here anyway." He nudged some papers on his desk. "I recall reading about the ambassador's death. The papers said nothing about missing diamonds, nor about any international art dealer and his

wife. Thieves broke in, shot the ambassador, presumably kidnapped his mistress, girl friend or what have
you." He turned abruptly to Tracy. "He says your husband engineered the robbery. Is that true?"

"Yes."

"You would sign a deposition to that effect?"

"Of course."

"Not that it would hold up in our court, but it would
give me something to take to my superiors." He turned
to Burt. "You understand that nearly everybody is at-
tending the disaster at Layou. The governor as well.
All communications are out, so it will be necessary for
me to drive up and get the necessary warrants. The
roads are washed out, but I should probably be back
late tomorrow."

Burt felt a cold fury pass through him, but he kept
his voice level. "Do you know Joss, Sergeant?"

"Of course. Quite a fascinating person—"

"She's on the island with two gunmen. They've already killed one of her boys. While we're sitting here
talking politely, making depositions, and going through
channels to make sure we don't get any demerits
against our next promotion, she could be dying."

The sergeant's face froze for an instant, his nostrils
flaring in anger. Abruptly he stood up, opened a
drawer, and took out a pistol in a button-down holster.
He clipped it to his belt, reached in another drawer and
took out a .32 automatic. He put it on the desk. "Take
it. Officially I didn't give it to you." He looked at
Tracy. "We'll take you by the hotel."

"I'm going."

Burt read in her eyes the fear of being alone. "Yes,
she goes with us."

Sergeant George sighed. "Life was simpler before I
became a sergeant anyway. Come on, you two. I'll req-
uisition a launch at the jetty."

"What if Rolf comes in at Grenada?" asked Burt.

Sergeant George clenched his jaw muscles, then
bowed to Burt in exaggerated politeness. "Thank you,

Sergeant, for your assistance. I shall radio the authorities their descriptions."

They started across the wide sweep of Kingstown harbor in a battered cabin cruiser which looked as though it had barely survived the Normandy landing. Burt, standing behind Sergeant George at the wheel, looked up through the port and saw a seaplane dropping down for a landing. "Where does it come from?"

"Trinidad, via Grenada." He looked at Burt. "You suppose they're on it?"

"Let's find out."

Their old cruiser made less than fifteen knots per hour. The floatplane had landed and a customs boat had pulled up alongside by the time they drew near. Burt peered through the window and saw Bunny step onto the customs boat. She looked chic and lovely in her smoke-blue suit.

"That's her," said Burt. "She's alone."

"I'll get her."

"She could be armed."

"Stay out of sight. I'll show you what official courtesy can do."

Burt watched through the porthole as Sergeant George stepped across to the customs boat, spoke a word to the officer, then bent his long body into a bow toward Bunny. She smiled and gave him her arm. He helped her onto the cruiser and opened the bulkhead door for her. Her eyes flew wide as she saw Burt and Tracy. She started to back out of the cabin and bumped into Sergeant George who blocked the door. She clawed open her purse, but Burt leaped forward and jerked it out of her hand. He lifted out a pearl-handled .32 and dropped it into his pocket.

"Where's Rolf?" asked Burt.

She showed her lovely white teeth in a sneer.

Burt shrugged. "Okay, you'll make me work for it." He turned to the sergeant. "Can you get us out into the harbor? I'll go on deck and have a talk with her."

When they were out in the harbor, Burt had her

standing facing the waist-high railing. She gave Burt a
half-smile over her shoulder. "You won't throw me
overboard, fuzz. I know you that well."

"I'll make you wish I had."

He stood for a moment thinking of how she'd tor-
tured him, of Joss and the boys at the mercy of Ace
and Hoke, and finally of her plan to take over Tracy's
life after she was dead. The last thought gave him the
will needed. With one swift movement he bent and
seized her ankles, lifted her, and pushed her forward
with his shoulder. She screamed as her head struck the
rushing water. Burt held to her silk-clad ankles as she
twisted and tried to raise herself. The skirt fell over her
head and he noted that she'd worn the black panties
decorated with kissing red lips. He counted to ten, then
pulled her back halfway across the railing. "Where's
Rolf?"

She coughed and sputtered. "Go to hell, you dirty—"

The water stopped her voice as he lowered her again.
This time he counted to twenty. When he pulled her
up, she collapsed on deck and threw up a gallon of sea
water.

"He's. . . coming in at Grenada . . ." she gasped finally. "He's got the man with him . . . the man with the
money. He planned to stop off for Tracy."

"Why?"

"To use her to . . . make you tell where you hid the
diamonds."

Back in the cabin, she slumped on the low bench
which ran across one wall. Burt told Sergeant George
what he'd learned.

"That counts him out," said the sergeant. "They'll
pick him up in Grenada. Now how do we get the others without getting Joss killed?"

Burt looked back along the low cabin. Tracy sat in a
corner with her knees under her chin, her gaudy dress
pulled down to her ankles. The faint trembling of her
shoulders told him she was fighting a silent private bat-
tle. Bunny sat across from her in the damp wrinkled
suit, her hair like a wet mop atop her skull. Her chic,

expensive look was gone; she now looked as beaten as
Tracy. Looking from one to the other, Burt was surprised to see how near Bunny had come to making herself a perfect copy of Tracy. He walked back and knelt
in front of Tracy. "There's something you could do,"
he said. "It's risky, but it might save the lives of five
other people."

She raised her head and regarded him gravely. "I'll
do anything you say. You should know that."

Her complete trust nearly caused him to abandon his
plan, but he had no other. "All right. Change clothes
with Bunny. You're going to be a decoy."

Bunny, with her shapeless polka dot dress a forecast
of less colorful but no less shapeless prison garb, was
left on Bequia in the custody of a corporal and his six-
by-six concrete jail. Sergeant George had exchanged his
uniform for the clothes of an island seaman: white canvas trousers cut off at the knees, a sleeveless undershirt,
and no shoes.

Burt watched the island draw near in the late afternoon sun. He was relieved to see nobody on the tower;
Ace's vigilance must have waned during the long days
of solitude. Burt directed Sergeant George to approach
the island from the west; the sun would be at their
backs, he explained, and a tongue of rocks screened the
sea from the clubhouse. He wrapped his gun in oilskin
and sat down to remove his sneakers. "I'll be behind
them in ten minutes. Tracy, just show your head and
shoulders above the cabin. Don't talk!"

"Yes, Burt." She knelt in the wrinkled suit, smelling
faintly of wet wool. She kissed him with lips that were
hot and cracked but strangely sweet. "Don't worry
about me. Take care of yourself."

He crawled to the side, slipped over into the water
and stroked silently along the rocks. He crawled out
onto a hidden patch of sand and unwrapped the gun
from its waterproof cocoon. Holding it in his right
hand, he crawled through the low bush until he was
twenty yards from the beach club. He could hear the
low grinding of the boat's diesel engine. He peered out

and saw Joss sitting on the steps of the beach club, her face like that of a robot which has been turned off. Coco lay in the sand with his hat over his eyes. Godfrey sat beside him and pulled ravelings from his frayed shorts. Hoke stood behind the bar, his shotgun resting on the polished wood and pointing at Joss's back. Ace walked down to the jetty, shading his eyes and peering toward the sound of the launch.

Burt watched the launch approach the break in the rocks; his stomach sank when he saw how vulnerable Tracy looked in Bunny's suit, like a small girl dressed up to play adult. Burt held his breath, then Ace called over his shoulder. "Okay, Hoke! It's Bunny."

The big man left the club and walked toward the beach. Burt waited until both men stood on the jetty, then he ran out in front of the club.

"You're covered, Ace! Don't move!"

As though it triggered a reflex action, Ace doubled over and swung his gun around. Before he completed the half-turn, Burt fired. Ace threw his arms wide and did a backflip off the jetty. Burt swung the gun to Hoke, who dropped the shotgun and raised his arms. Burt walked forward and looked down at Ace. A redness oozed from his chest and tinted the crystalline water a delicate pink. The gentle surf rocked his lifeless head from side to side as though he were saying, in a slow, tired manner, no . . . no . . . no . . .

"Burt!" Joss seized his neck and shouted in his ear. "They said you were dead. When you jumped in front of me, I thought . . . good God! I've *really* wigged out now."

Sergeant George nosed the launch up to the jetty; Burt helped him tie Hoke and lay him in the cabin. Joss invited everybody to the club for drinks, and Burt remembered the diamonds.

"I'll join you later," he said.

Tracy ran up and seized his hand. "You don't leave me, remember?"

They walked along the path, past cabins four, three, and two. "Where are we going?" she asked.

"To a certain cave—"

He stopped, frozen. Rolf had stepped out from behind the banyan with the gun leveled in his fist.

"Don't move, Burt. She gets the first shot. Tracy, take that gun from his pocket and bring it to me."

She hesitated, and Burt licked his dry lips. A burst of Joss's half-hysterical laughter came from the direction of the club.

"Do as he says," Burt told her.

She delivered the gun to Rolf, who dropped it in his pocket. He caught her arm and pulled her in front of him. "All right, Burt. Take me to the diamonds."

"You won't hurt her?"

"You're in a poor bargaining position, but . . ." he shrugged. "Show me the diamonds and she goes unharmed."

Burt led the way across the crusted grass. He remembered the last time he had made this trip, with Ace and Hoke behind him. He had known they would kill him; he was not certain about Rolf. The man could kill on a momentary whim, true, but a similar whim could stop him from killing. Rolf was logical in his own way; perhaps the diamonds would be enough. . . .

"They were watching for you in Grenada," he said. "What happened?"

"I saw them before they saw me. They weren't watching for a man carrying a baby." Rolf chuckled. "It pays to be chivalrous. My companion wasn't, and he got caught."

Burt climbed down the low cliff and started along the pebble beach. He heard Rolf's voice behind him:

"Something like old home week, isn't it, Tracy? I presume he took you off the island. Has he been treating you well?"

"Better than you ever did."

"Isn't that sweet?"

Burt heard a low grunt of pain. He turned to see Tracy fall forward onto her hands. He clenched his fists and took a step forward. Rolf pressed the gun against the back of her neck.

"Come on, March. Come and get her killed."

Burt stopped, trembling with suppressed rage. "You only get one shot, Rolf. Then I'll kill you with my bare hands."

"Ah, the beast is out, is it?"

"It will be if you kill her."

"What if I kill you first?"

"You never find the diamonds."

Rolf nodded slowly. "Beautiful. Beautiful impasse. I like you for an enemy, Burt." He straightened. "Get up, Tracy."

When they were walking again, Rolf said, "You must have had an interesting time on the island, Tracy. Plans for the future and all that. Will he be your connection? It won't be hard for a cop."

"I don't use it any more."

His only answer was laughter.

Burt walked along the low cliff, thinking fast and getting nowhere. He could have escaped easily, but the fact that Rolf had Tracy made it useless. He couldn't depend on Rolf not to kill her. . . .

Burt saw the lamplight before he entered the cave, but Maudie wasn't there. She must have heard the launch coming and run up to the hills. Burt turned as Tracy came in, followed by Rolf.

"Where are they?"

"Let her walk out of here first," said Burt. "When she's out from under the gun, I'll show you."

Rolf's teeth showed like fangs in the lamplight. "You picked a poor time for an ultimatum, Burt. The diamonds are here?" His eyes flicked around the cave. "Sure. This is that girl's rathole. Over there, both of you." He shoved Tracy over beside Burt and had them both squat down with their hands clasped above their heads. Then he rummaged swiftly through Maudie's trove of treasures. Finding nothing, he started checking each crevice in the cave wall. The gun never left Tracy's heart; Burt was watching it.

"We made a deal, Rolf. I thought you always fulfilled your contracts, even with Nazis."

"Technically," said Rolf, "you have taken me to the diamonds, though I don't have them yet. And technically I am fulfilling my contract. I haven't killed Tracy—yet."

Burt's heart sank. "Why should you kill her?"

"Because I can."

"Then it's as good as done, isn't it?"

Rolf frowned, tugging at the rock Burt had jammed against the box. "You sound as though you have a point to make."

"I mean," said Burt, "you'd be getting a sitting duck. There'd be no problem in killing her, a little touch on the trigger and the machine stops. Click. She's dead, and there's no more kick than shutting off a radio."

"Maybe to you—"

"To you, too. Man, I know this score. Half the kick is anticipation, the other half is danger. Getting the other guy before he gets you. You think you're unique in this world? Rolf Keener, the incomparable killer? You and a hundred thousand Nazis, you and Caligula, you and probably a billion others since the beginning of time. You go around shutting other people off because you see yourselves in them, and you hate what you see."

"You see yourself in me?"

"Sure."

"You hate me?"

"I understand you. That cancels out the rest of it."

Rolf's lip curled. "You want to take me in and be a character witness for me?"

"I want you to take the diamonds and go."

"Suppose I were caught—"

"I'd do all I could to see you fry."

Rolf laughed. "That's better, Burt. I thought you were about to come on with violin music. Ah!" He pulled out the strongbox. Burt rocked forward on his feet, and Rolf's gun boomed like thunder in the cave. A rock fragment gouged Burt's cheek.

"Sit tight, Burt. We haven't finished our talk."

Rolf spun the combination, opened the strongbox,

and glanced at the glittering fortune nestled in velvet. With his left hand he began stuffing the diamonds in his pocket. When one pocket was full, he shifted the gun and began filling the other. To make room, he took out Burt's gun and dropped it behind him. To Burt he said: "You seemed about to suggest another deal. What was it?"

"A hand-to-hand fight. Winner take all."

Rolf laughed. "You always suggest that when you're at my mercy. I'm already the winner." He finished emptying the strongbox and stood up. "Let's put it up to Tracy. Tracy, you want to stay and die with him, or you want to live with me?"

Tracy gasped. "You mean, Burt—"

"He lives—if you come with me."

She looked at Burt, and he read the anguish in her eyes. "Decide for yourself," he said.

"I did that a week ago. I'd rather die than live with him."

"Then that's your answer."

"Look here, Tracy, before you decide." Rolf squatted on his heels and opened his palm. Inside it was a small white capsule.

She gasped. "No!"

"You could sniff it right here. Right now."

"I don't . . . want it."

Rolf moved his hand, and the capsule landed at her feet. She stared down at it, trembling, the sweat beading her brow. Rolf spoke softly:

"You just imagine you've kicked the habit. You really haven't. You'll go back to it sooner or later. Why go through a lot of pain—?"

Burt saw his chance and lunged between Rolf and Tracy. The gun boomed, and the bullet ripped through his upper arm like a lance of fire. Burt drove his knee into Rolf's face and knocked him backward. He leaped on Rolf and ground his knee into the other's throat. He seized the wrist of Rolf's gun-hand in both of his, hammering the knuckles against the rock until the fingers gave up the gun. Burt seized it just as Rolf arched his back and threw him off. Burt rose to see Rolf lunge out of the cave. Burt ran out behind him and saw him wading through the black water.

"Stop!" he shouted.

"Shoot me," yelled Rolf.

Burt fired, and his bullet struck sparks from the rock beside Rolf's head. Rolf left the crevice and turned right. Burt followed and saw that Rolf had walked out on a blind ledge, fifteen feet above the rocky beach. He stood with his back to the wall, his face smeared with blood.

"All right, Rolf," said Burt. "Come on back."

Rolf threw back his head and laughed. "You'll have to shoot me."

"The state handles executions."

"They don't have the right! A bunch of moronic electricians, what have they done? *They* didn't beat me. You did. So shoot!"

Burt started edging toward him.

"Your gun isn't much good, is it?" Rolf laughed and leaped headfirst off the ledge. Burt thought he'd decided to dash out his brains on the rocks, but the lean body knifed the water three feet beyond the rocks and came up swimming. Burt saw the power cruiser riding at anchor a hundred yards out. He felt a curdling anger in his stomach; Rolf had been sure he wouldn't shoot. Now Rolf was getting away; the old diesel could never catch him.

Burt dived out over the rocks, thankful that the beach was narrower here; he struck the water, arched his back, and came up swimming with all his strength. He saw that he was slowly closing the gap. Thirty feet, twenty . . .

A twinge in his arm reminded him of the wound. Losing blood . . . He heard Tracy's distant scream. He glanced over his shoulder to see a huge dorsal fin knifing through the water. Tiger shark, he thought in panic, must have been nosing around the rocks. He saw the fin turn sideways as the monster twisted for the bite. Burt surfaced, dived, and clawed for depth. He glimpsed a bulking shadow above him, then a huge body like a stucco wall slammed against him and sent him spinning down into the depths. He rose slowly, watching for the monster's second pass. It didn't come, and Burt saw why. Rolf was sinking down through the sunbeams that speared the air-clear water, turning slowly over and over. It was an oddly foreshortened Rolf, ending at his hips. Each stump gave forth a blue fountain which turned to red and drifted away like tenuous pink veils. The impossibly huge bulk of the shark returned, and the scene dissolved into churning red froth. Burt turned and stroked rapidly back to shore.

Tracy was waiting on the rocky beach. "Rolf—?"

"He's dead."

She lowered her head and looked at the capsule in her palm. "I've been holding this, fighting with myself . . ."

"Yes?" said Burt. "Who won?"

"There are no winners," she said. She tossed the capsule into a pool of water trapped by the rocks. Together they watched the ripples spread out and disappear.

Ⓢ

Other Mysteries from SIGNET

☐ **KILLER'S PAYOFF by Ed McBain.** A blackmailer who'd gone too far, Sy Kramer had earned his last payoff, a bullet in the head! Which of Kramer's pigeons had so much at stake that murder seemed a good gamble? The boys of the 87th had to find the desperate killer before he or she struck again.   (#Q5939—95¢)

☐ **KISS THE BOYS AND MAKE THEM DIE by James Yardley.** A lovely lady agent and her tough ex-cop boss chase across the Middle East in this fast-paced suspense thriller of international intrigue. (#Q5554—95¢)

☐ **COP HATER by Ed McBain.** He was swift, silent and deadly—and knocking off the 87th Precinct's finest, one by one. If Steve Carella didn't find the cop killer soon he might find himself taking a cool trip to the morgue!
                                                     (#Q5617—95¢)

☐ **THE VENUS PROBE by E. Howard Hunt.** Peter Ward sets out on a round-the-world manhunt to find the thread linking the disappearance of seven internationally known scientists.   (#Q5782—95¢)

☐ **FUZZ by Ed McBain.** A homemade bomb, a couple of fun-loving youngsters and an ingenious extortion scheme add up to big excitement.   (#T5151—75¢)

☐ **FESTIVAL FOR SPIES by E. Howard Hunt.** Peter Ward, CIA agent, foils an insidious plot to pull Cambodia into the Chinese Communist orbit.   (#Q5781—95¢)

THE NEW AMERICAN LIBRARY, INC.,
P.O. Box 999, Bergenfield, New Jersey 07621

Please send me the SIGNET BOOKS I have checked above. I am enclosing $_____(check or money order—no currency or C.O.D.'s). Please include the list price plus 25¢ a copy to cover handling and mailing costs. (Prices and numbers are subject to change without notice.)

Name_____

Address_____

City_____State_____Zip Code_____
Allow at least 3 weeks for delivery